HER DEEPEST FEAR

A ROSEMARY RUN THRILLER

KELLY UTT

2019 Standards of Starlight Paperback Edition

www.standardsofstarlight.com

ISBN: 978-1-7337712-7-6

Cover art by Justin Carolyne

PROLOGUE

It had been an ordinary autumn day, right up until Cate Brady's police-officer brother knocked on the door of her Northern California home to deliver the most horrific news. Cate wanted to collapse into a ball on her living room floor when the terrible words reached her ears, piercing and slicing into her very soul, but doing so was out of the question. The kids were watching.

Instead, Cate wrung the blue and white striped dishtowel in her hands as she looked at her brother, Officer James Tatum, in disbelief. She smoothed the cotton fabric down hard, as if the movement could somehow steady her. Tears filled her eyes and burned like hot coals searing their way down her cheeks. She felt dizzy. *How could this be?*

Cate and her children had eaten homemade pizza for dinner and were busy cleaning up the mess together when James knocked. Her teenage son, Aaron, remained at the sink, his earbuds blasting classic rock music while he absentmindedly scrubbed and rinsed dishes, waiting for his mom to return to her drying duties. Cate's middle child, Jilly, and the baby of the family, Niko, both stood near the dinner table, clearing away dirty napkins and wiping crumbs off the smooth, flat surface.

Cate almost had it all. The picture-perfect house. The well-balanced, adoring kids. The friendly extended family members who lived nearby. The glamorous job traveling around the wine country region and writing lifestyle pieces for the local magazine. And the storybook marriage to a man who worked hard to provide for her every want and need. When his day at the office was done, Mick Brady typically came home to help cook dinner, play with the kids, and watch television in bed before wrapping his arms around his wife and falling peacefully asleep with the family's yellow lab, Mcesha, at his feet.

Cate had waited many years for the life she enjoyed now, having traipsed around the world while living in one temporary rental home after another when Mick was an officer in the U.S. Navy. Mick had promised his wife a beautiful place to put down roots once he retired from active duty service. And he delivered on that promise. Rosemary Run felt like home.

But fate had other plans which rudely interrupted this ordinary day and disrupted Cate's idyllic life.

James choked up as he told his sister the news: Mick had been in an accident. He was pronounced dead on the scene.

C ate's hands trembled as she stared at the mound of dirt piled neatly beside her husband's flag-draped casket. None of this felt real. The medical examiner said Mick's body was badly mangled, so she had decided not to see it, but one look at her grieving children told Cate this was very real.

The air was much colder than usual on this particular morning. So cold that Cate had spent the evening prior digging out warm clothes for her family to wear to the funeral and interment. The warm clothes had been packed away since moving from Mick's last duty station. It was lucky they still fit, save for a few inconspicuous tight seams and short hems.

Maybe the weather had something to do with why this all felt to Cate like a strange dream. It shouldn't have been so cold in Rosemary Run. Not in October. Temperatures like these were better suited for higher elevations and points north. Cate pondered the strangeness of her reality as she looked slowly from the mound of dirt to each of her kids, assessing their levels of distress, one by one. She thought about how none of them would ever forget this dreadful day. Her sweet, innocent kids would be scarred forever. They'd never be the same.

Niko sat nearby to where Cate was standing, bundled up in long pants and a cable-knit sweater. His hair was brushed purposefully to one side. Cate thought he suddenly looked awfully grown-up for five. No child his age should have to face such an unexpected and profound loss. Niko's Uncle James sat in the seat next to him, one arm draped around the top of the little boy's chair.

James' pretty, red-headed wife, Rebecca, dabbed her eyes with a silk handkerchief as she sat dutifully on the other side and leaned close against her husband to keep warm. Being the wife of a police officer, Rebecca had been to more funerals than she could count. But this one was different. Burying a beloved family member was excruciating for everyone involved. She worked hard to maintain her composure. Rebecca and James didn't have kids of their own yet. They wanted desperately to help take good care of their niece and nephews.

Jilly sat huddled beside her baby brother and stared blankly at the pile of dirt, fixing her gaze on the same spot as her mom. She had wanted to wear her nicest black dress, which fell just above her knee, so she'd added warm leggings underneath to accommodate the blustery conditions. In typical tween-girl fashion, she had taken extra time with her clothes and appearance. Ever since the weather turned, it was Jilly who had cursed the cold most of all. She'd never liked wintertime and found it especially cruel that such bitter cold would arrive on the day of her father's funeral.

Aaron had decided to stand up and remain next to his mother's side, taking to heart what his Uncle James had said about being strong. It was too much to ask of a freshman in high school. He fidgeted with the collar of his starched, white dress shirt and adjusted the blue tie around his neck. It had been his dad's. Cate's heart felt like it was breaking right inside of her as she thought about how Mick had looked forward to Aaron wearing one of his ties for a special occasion. He had considered it an important rite of passage. Surely, Mick never dreamed his boy would be wearing this tie while standing at his graveside on this unimaginable day. The very thought would have turned Mick inside out. He loved his children most of all.

Cate wondered how everything could go so wrong. Especially after life had seemed so perfectly right.

Little more than a year ago, the Brady family had been living in Connecticut. Mick's position as an officer at the Naval Submarine Base New London in Groton had kept him away from home a lot, but they were used to it. The facility was the primary submarine base on the East Coast. The men and women stationed there had important jobs to do. That fact made Mick's absence easier for Cate and the kids to accept, even though they didn't like it.

Cate used to beg Mick to retire from the service so he could spend more time with her and the kids. Now, she wished she'd never been so selfish. She imagined her husband would still be alive if they'd never moved home. Mick would have been gone too much, for sure. But, at least, he'd always return. Not to mention, she and the kids would have had their old friends around.

It was hard for Cate not to feel like this was all her fault.

"Ma'am," an officiant said to Cate as he gently placed a hand on her arm. "It's time for the riflemen to fire the ceremonial three volleys. I don't want the sound to startle you. Are you and your children ready?"

Cate nodded. She had explained to Aaron, Jilly, and Niko about the volleys and how they were fired at Navy military funerals. She'd also told them about how Taps would be played by a military bugler after the firing of the volleys, just before the American flag was taken off the top of their father's casket, then folded and presented to his family.

But Cate wasn't ready. Not really. She wasn't ready to say goodbye to the only man she'd ever truly loved. She wasn't ready to grow old without him. Or to raise their three children alone. She wasn't ready for any of this. She wished she could somehow rewind time and change something that would bring him back.

Cate wanted to smell Mick's aftershave and the way it mixed with the scent of his bath soap as he stepped out of the shower each morning, clean and refreshed. She wanted to hear his cheerful voice as he announced his arrival after a long day of work. She wanted to see his Sunday newspaper, sprawled about on the kitchen counter with the comics on top. And she wanted to feel his familiar touch as he clasped her hand in his, like he'd done so many times over their sixteen years together. She wanted to be Cate and Mick. Mick and Cate. It had been printed on their wedding announcements when they married young, and on countless holiday cards, party invitations, and permission slips over the years since. They were barely twenty and twenty-one when they had wed. People had told them they were foolish and that their union would never last. But it had. Cate didn't know who to be in the world if not a part of Mick. She felt completely and utterly alone.

At a loss, both figuratively and literally, Cate turned to her kids and said, "it's time."

"Okay, Mommy," Niko replied feebly as he nodded his little head up and down. Both Jilly and Aaron were too choked up to speak.

"We're ready," Cate confirmed, signaling the officiant to go ahead.

Tears streamed down her face as Cate stood tall and braced herself for the booms. She held her head high, though she cried silently, careful not to let the kids hear her sobbing out loud. She *had* to be strong for them.

Each boom felt like a punch to the gut as it came, pushing Cate deeper and deeper into a future she didn't want and couldn't escape. Her heart raced. It felt like the sounds were sealing the lid of her own coffin. The bugler played his slow, sorrowful tune while Cate began to dread the impending moment when Mick's casket would be lowered into the unforgiving ground. She thought about how it was even colder down there. She suddenly had the overwhelming urge to race over to her husband, fling his casket open, and hold him in her arms a while longer. She wanted to save him from the ground. She wanted to save herself.

Finally, the last three notes of Taps escaped from the bugler's instrument into the cold October air, the closing one held and left to echo throughout what seemed like the entire valley. As is customary, the body bearers carefully removed the flag from Mick's casket, then folded it thirteen times into a triangle. Mark Boche, a long-time shipmate of Mick's who had flown in from Connecticut for the funeral, dutifully presented the flag to Cate as he leaned towards her. The flag felt heavy and cumbersome in her hands. She appreciated the honor shown to her husband, but the reality of his fate was something she didn't want to face. Even as Mick's casket was lowered, slowly, into the ground.

In a spontaneous move, Cate jerked her body around in her chair to look away. When she did, her eyes landed on a shadowy figure just beyond the tree line at the edge of the cemetery. She couldn't quite make out whether it was a man or a woman, but *someone* was there. Someone was watching.

Realizing they had been spotted, the figure darted behind a large oak tree, then scrambled further into the woods, out of sight.

"Can I get you something, kiddo?"

James was four years older and often called his little sister "kiddo." He had started when they were very young, probably in an attempt to appear wise and mature. It remained as a term of endearment.

"How about a stiff drink?" Cate replied, only half joking. Mourners would arrive at her home any moment now. They'd all want to talk with her. And she was exhausted.

James chuckled.

"I don't think that's the best idea, sis." Another term of endearment. "How about a glass of tea?"

"Fine," Cate replied. "I guess that will have to do."

She wanted to tell her brother about the stranger in the woods. Until she saw the figure along the tree line, it hadn't occurred to Cate that Mick's death might not have been an accident. She wondered if there was more to the story. Most of all, she wondered if she and the kids might be in danger.

"Say," Cate began. "Why did we host at my house, anyway? Shouldn't the grieving widow be afforded a little peace and quiet?"

"You're right," Rebecca chimed in. "We should be at our house right now. Not yours. Do you want me to redirect people there? Because I could."

"Oh, nonsense," Cate insisted, backpedaling. "It's too late for that. I'm just thinking out loud. I don't mean for you to do anything, Bec. You've done enough already."

Jilly sat on the sofa next to Rebecca as her aunt gently stroked the back of her curly brown hair. Niko was positioned on the other side, napping with his head in his aunt's lap. It was a perfect illustration of just how helpful Rebecca had been. She was a good sister-in-law. Cate wholeheartedly approved of James' choice of a spouse. Not to mention, she thought Rebecca would make a wonderful mother someday.

"You know we love you and these kids, don't you?" Rebecca asked, talking quietly so as not to wake Niko. "James and I would do anything for you. Just say the word and we'll make sure it's done."

"I know," Cate confirmed. "I promise I do. I'm a mess right now. I don't even know what I need."

Though, she thought about how she needed to find out who had been watching from the woods. Cate told herself there would be time for that inquiry, later.

Her thoughts wandered back to the day her husband died. Mick rarely missed an evening meal, which made it especially odd that he didn't call to let her know he wouldn't be home on that particular evening. James said Mick had been killed around seven o'clock. But Cate wondered what had happened in the hours prior that kept him from phoning. She wanted to search through his text and email records. She wanted to feel useful.

"Here you go," her brother said, his hand outstretched with a glass of tea. "Just the way you like it, half sweet and half unsweet."

James had snapped Cate back to reality just in time because two cars were pulling into the driveway.

"Thank you," she said.

"I still find it funny how attached you are to that sweet tea," James continued. "It tastes like syrup to me."

"To me, too," Rebecca added. "How did you come to like sweetened tea, anyway?"

"Oh, I first tried sweet tea when we were stationed at Kings Bay in Georgia," Cate said. "People drink it like hummingbirds on nectar down there. I became a convert. I drink it half-and-half to try and keep my sugar intake at a reasonable level. But the full sugar version is heavenly, especially when it's first brewed."

Cate found it odd to be talking about something as mundane as tea, but she didn't know what else to do with herself. After all, what was the alternative? Should she have mentioned that she wasn't even sure how Mick died? Or how she worried about being able to afford the family's beautiful home without his income?

Before James could sit back down and join them on the sofa, the first few guests had gotten out of their cars and were knocking on the front door. Meesha galloped dutifully to check out the newcomers. She took her guard dog responsibilities seriously.

Cate hoped the pup would cope well with having a

house full of people. It was sure to be a large crowd, larger than they had ever welcomed before, and Meesha seemed to be having a hard time with Mick's absence. For the past few nights, she had been lying in her usual spot at the bottom of his side of the bed, whining softly. She was grieving, too.

Cate found herself surprised at how the little things had been catching her off guard since her husband died. She expected to be upset by the big things. But some of the simplest, mundane situations were doing a number on her. Like that morning, when she had gotten in the family's minivan to drive to the funeral. Mick had driven the van last, so the seat was adjusted to accommodate his long legs. A wave of sadness washed over Cate as she pushed the button to move the seat forward, knowing she'd be doing so for the last time. None of this was fair.

"Hello, everybody," James and Cate's mom, Ellen Tatum, said as she walked through the door. Their dad, Ron Tatum, followed close behind.

Ellen was a spunky woman. She was the librarian at the town elementary school and had an enthusiasm for life not common in women her age. Cate always thought how her mom should have been involved in theater. She had a flair for the dramatic that would surely have served her well on stage.

Always fashionable, Ellen arrived dressed in a crisp a-line skirt and a silky blouse. She wore a wool coat over top, which looked like she had purchased special for the occasion. Cate thought that made sense, what with the cold weather and all. Ellen's hair landed just above her shoulders and was professionally colored a warm chestnut brown. She looked great for a woman in her late fifties. So good, in fact, that it wasn't unusual for her and Cate to be confused for sisters.

"Mom," Cate said, glad to see her mother. "You look great. Is your coat new?"

"It is," Ellen replied. "Luckily, my favorite department store had it in stock. I thought I might have had to go on a quick jaunt to Sacramento to find something to wear in this cold. But Decker's came through for me at the last minute."

"Jilly, dear," Cate said, turning towards her daughter. "Doesn't your grandmother's new coat look pretty?"

Jilly nodded. She seemed to have heard the words, although Cate wasn't sure she was processing.

"Sacramento is a long way to go for a coat," James said, kissing his mother on the cheek and welcoming her in.

"Come now, James," Cate said to her brother. "You know how important fashion is to Mom. I could see her making the trip."

"Oh, I understand completely," Rebecca echoed, following her husband's kiss on Ellen's cheek with one of her own. Rebecca loved her mother-in-law. They got along better than most. And she shared Ellen's love of fashion.

Ron Tatum was a few years older than his wife, but he looked every bit as youthful, even in his early sixties. He was a telephone lineman by trade, and he kept himself in peak physical condition. He always said that being in shape helped him to stay safe while doing his job. His dedication to good health and physical fitness was about to pay off because he was set to retire in three short years and had plans to do all sorts of outdoor activities in his free time. Cate could easily imagine him kayaking on the river, hiking the rolling hills which surrounded the valley and tending to his backyard vegetable garden. Ron's hair was an attractive salt and pepper gray, cut short and neat. He wore a charcoal color suit with a black tie. He cleaned up well. So well, that you would never guess he worked as a lineman if you saw him all dressed up this way.

"Come in, Dad," Cate said as she reached her arms out to hug her father. "You look good. You sure do you clean up nice."

"All the Tatum men do," Ron said, winking at his son.

"Don't you mean the Tatum *and* the Brady men?" Aaron asked from the other side of the room. It was an innocent question, but a telling one. The poor kid was missing his father something fierce.

"You're exactly right, my boy," Ron said, hurrying over to embrace his grandson. Cate knew she could count on her dad to step in and fill some roles Mick was leaving behind. She was grateful to be living near family, for this reason, most of all.

"You just saw us at the cemetery," Ellen said to her daughter. "You're complimenting our outfits as if we hadn't seen each other earlier today."

"Forgive me," Cate replied. "I know I was standing there at the cemetery, but my mind was a million miles away. I think I was just gritting my teeth and bearing it, hoping for the graveside service to be over as quickly as possible. And besides, I couldn't focus on much else besides the pile of cold dirt and my husband's casket."

Cate teared up as she said these words to her mother. She had cried for what seemed like hours already that day and she had promised herself that she would stop to socialize with the guests who were coming to her home. She intended to stop. But her emotions got the best of her as salty water streamed down her cheeks. There was another knock on the front door, so Cate quickly dried her eyes and tried to look normal.

James opened the door, playing the part of host even though this was his sister's house. Cate appreciated his efforts and was happy to let him take the lead. Meesha ran to his side, apparently knowing that the next guests were not members of the immediate family. It was time for Cate to put on her game face.

Sean O'Brien looked cheerful as he and his grandson stood on the Brady family's doorstep, freshly baked cookies in hand. He looked almost too cheerful, like he was attending a game night instead of a wake. His grandson, Mitchell, stood at his side, looking shy. Mitchell was close to Jilly's age, and they both attended the same middle school in town. Cate wasn't sure they had ever formally met, but she'd noticed there were lots of awkward silences when Jilly and Mitchell would pass each other in the neighborhood. Sean had lived in Rosemary Run for years, but his grandson had only recently joined him after his father-- Sean's son-- had passed away and his drug-addicted mother had been sent to jail. Perhaps it was his family's checkered past that made him shy.

"Sean, thanks for coming," Cate said as she took the plate of cookies out of his hand. "And Mitchell, good to see you, too, young man."

"We wouldn't miss it," Sean said, again seeming a little too eager. He noticed his tone this time and tried once more, clearing his throat. "I'm very sorry for your loss, Mrs. Brady. Mitchell and I made these cookies for you and the kids ourselves."

Rosemary Run was the kind of town where everyone knew your business. Sean seemed friendly enough, though Cate thought he might have a little too much time on his hands. She could imagine him being nosy and prying into things she'd rather he didn't know about. She decided to put the focus on the kids.

"Jilly, honey," she called out to her daughter. "Mitchell O'Brien is here. Why don't you come say hello?"

Jilly looked visibly uncomfortable at the suggestion, but she followed her mother's instructions. She knew it would be necessary to remain involved with the events of today, even if she didn't want to. She figured she might as well cooperate.

Sean was a widower who lost his wife a few years prior. It suddenly occurred to Cate just how many people had lost loved ones in this town. She had heard their stories before, but they had seemed distant and remote. Now, the harsh realities her fellow neighbors already knew had arrived, unwelcome, at her own front door.

Sean stepped inside the house as another car pulled in the driveway to take his place in what Cate imagined would be an endless line of people arriving throughout the afternoon. This time, it was her friend Sasha Lansing from the magazine. She had brought her husband with her. And she looked almost embarrassed to have a happy marriage and a spouse.

"Cate, darling," Sasha said as she stepped out of her full-size SUV and rushed over to give her friend a hug. She didn't even look back to see if her husband was behind her.

Cate suddenly felt embarrassed because Sasha was embarrassed. Cate hoped that her friends wouldn't treat her any differently now that she was a widow. She hated even thinking that word to herself. It reminded her of an old spinster, lonesome and bitter.

"Thank you for coming," Cate said as she embraced her friend. "You know, you don't have to treat me any differently. I'm still the same old Cate Brady."

As the words came out of Cate's mouth, she knew she wasn't the same. She wanted to be, but the fact was, she would never be the same ever again. Maybe people *should* treat her differently. She had no idea how to act.

"Oh, I know," Sasha said convincingly. "I'm just so sorry about what happened. Mick was such a good man. He was a wonderful father to the kids and a great husband to you. I know you must be devastated."

And so began the seemingly endless well wishes which usually made Cate feel worse rather than better. She understood that people were trying to be kind and to make her feel loved. Most often, though, their words only made her feel worse. Like Sasha's. Of course, Cate was devastated. She wondered why Sasha needed to say those words, driving the point deeper.

Sasha's husband, Todd Talbot, exited their vehicle and scurried along behind his wife. He, too, looked embarrassed to be part of a happy marriage. He looked uncomfortable in his skin, like he thought he should apologize for staying alive.

Cate and Sasha had attended elementary school together. They went way back, much farther than being coworkers at the magazine. They'd lost touch during some years Cate was away, but they'd kept up with each other on social media and had fallen right back into a comfortable friendship when Cate moved home. Cate thought, of all the people, Sasha and Todd would be a couple she could count on for support. She never imagined they would suddenly start acting strange around her. She wondered if this would go on indefinitely or if things would get back to normal between them after a certain period of time.

Cate ushered her friends inside the house and remained on the porch because she saw members of Mick's family who had flown in from Oklahoma arriving in their rental car.

Mick's mother, Nancy, was a nasty old woman. She saw fit to criticize anyone who came into her view, whether that be a stranger in a public place or her closest family members in private. Mick had distanced himself from his family of origin because of Nancy's behavior. Aaron, Jilly, and Niko had hardly known her. Cate wished she didn't have to face Nancy today, but it had seemed only right that the woman be allowed to attend her son's funeral.

Cate thought Nancy looked a lot like a fairytale villain as she eyeballed her inside the car. Nancy had jet black hair, large costume jewelry, high heels, and a fur coat. Her dye job looked severe and unnatural. It wasn't nearly as nice as Ellen's.

Mick's father had passed away when he was a boy, but Al DeAngelo, his stepdad, had entered the picture not long after and had been a positive influence in Mick's life as he grew up. Al was a New York transplant brought to Oklahoma by a job working on the railroad. He maintained his thick Brooklyn accent, which Cate had always found charming. Al was a good guy. He was nice to be around. Cate always wondered what he saw in Nancy.

As Cate waved to her in-laws, she made a silent wish for Nancy to somehow tone down her behavior during this visit. Or, at least, for Al to place himself front and center, so he'd fill the air time, leaving Nancy without a chance to get too many digs in. Cate felt like she couldn't take being heavily criticized right now. She felt weak and vulnerable and wasn't in the mood for Nancy's usual onslaught. Most of all, she thought her kids couldn't take it. Cate decided right then and there she would not let Nancy say anything disrespectful to her children. They were grieving the loss of their father and were rattled to the core. They didn't need to deal with nastiness on this of all days.

"Hi there, doll," Al said. Coming from anyone else, Cate might have thought being called doll was an insult. But she understood that, for Al, it was used in a friendly and affectionate way. Maybe it was his Brooklyn roots showing through.

"Hello, Al," she said with a smile. Then flatly, "Nancy."

Cate struggled to smile at her mother-in-law. She

wasn't successful. There was bad blood between Nancy and Mick, and Cate wouldn't soon forget it.

The pair climbed the steps onto Cate's porch silently. For her part, Cate was happy to send them on inside for someone else to deal with. James knew the dynamics well. Hopefully, he and Rebecca would take the lead in providing a buffer between the in-laws and the kids.

Cate remained on the porch for what felt like a long while as she greeted guest after guest. When the house was finally full and bursting at the seams, she stepped inside and did her best forced-smile facade of happiness as she spoke with each person who had taken the time to show up in person and wish her well. It was every bit as exhausting as she had expected, yet at the same time, a comfort. Cate would take all the comfort she could get.

3

By the time everyone but family went home, Cate, Aaron, Jilly, and Niko were spent. They were grateful to have made it through so much of the day and were looking forward to climbing into bed when it was done. But first, it was time for dinner. James offered to order pizza so they could relax together without having to cook. Even if he hadn't, enough casseroles had been delivered to last them the rest of the week.

Much to Cate's chagrin, Nancy and Al decided to hang around for dinner. Nancy had been on her best behavior so far, but Cate suspected that her claws would come out soon. It simply wasn't possible for Nancy to spend any length of time around others without unwelcome comments.

As Cate watched her brother fumble for a phone number and jot down pizza orders, she wondered if Mick had ever thought about his own death. She wondered whether he had thought about what would happen to his family after he was gone. Just last week, Mick had looked at the empty refrigerator and made a bad joke about how someone needed to die around there to get the fridge properly stocked with food. Cate wondered if some part of him knew what was coming.

As everyone chatted and waited for dinner, Aaron made a special effort to be friendly to his grandparents. He seemed to have extra sympathy for Nancy. Cate supposed Aaron had a few good memories of his grandmother and wanted to give her a chance. He surely remembered her more than his younger siblings because Mick and Cate had taken him around Nancy when he was little. They had rolled things back when Aaron was about the age Niko was now. Jilly and Niko had hardly spent any time around their grandmother at all. Truth be told, they knew the cashiers at the grocery store better.

"Grandma Nancy," Aaron began. "Would you like to play some cards with me? I remember that you liked to play. I've gotten pretty good at rummy."

Before answering, Nancy turned and looked at her husband excitedly. She appeared to be happy the kid was attempting to interact with her. Cate thought, for a fleeting moment, that maybe there was some humanity in Nancy yet. Though she quickly dismissed the thought as unlikely.

"Yes, Aaron, I would," Nancy replied. Her voice was scratchy. Too many years of chain-smoking cigarettes had given her a husky voice Cate thought could never quite return to normal.

Aaron cleared off the coffee table and went to get the playing cards from his room. Nancy scooted an armchair up close and leaned over, ready to play. It looked like a normal interaction between a grandparent and her grandson, but Cate was waiting for the other shoe to drop. Having Nancy here made her tense. Cate absentmindedly twirled and pulled at small sections of her hair as she sat on the sofa nearby. She thought to herself that if she could just get through this evening, life would move on. She'd go back to work and the kids would go back to school. It would be difficult and horrible to move forward without Mick, however, right now the thought of a daily routine made Cate feel hopeful.

"It's very kind of you to ask your grandmother to play cards," Al said to Aaron with a smile as the boy returned to the living room, cards in hand. "She seems rough, but inside that harsh exterior is a woman who has feelings just like the rest of us. She cares about you kids. This means a lot to her."

Cate tried not to roll her eyes.

Nancy sat up straight and bristled at Al's words. She appeared to be doing her best to hold her frustrations in.

Aaron smiled, innocently, and nodded his head. He said nothing because he didn't know exactly what to say. He was still an awkward teenage boy.

"Maybe when we're done playing cards, we can watch a movie in the den, too," Aaron said eagerly. He was trying to extend a welcome to his grandmother and to extend what he thought would be fun. Cate wasn't so sure she wanted the old woman to be around that late into the evening. Cate glanced at her brother, who could tell what she was thinking.

"I'm not sure there will be enough time for that this

evening, buddy," James said to his nephew so his sister didn't have to. "Maybe another time."

"That's right," Cate echoed. "We need to get to bed. We've all had a long day. Besides, I thought you wanted to go back to school in the morning."

"I did," Aaron confirmed. "But if Grandma and Al can stay, maybe I'll skip one more day. They could come back to our house tomorrow."

Cate's stomach tightened at the thought of it. She wanted to get rid of them and fast, before Aaron got too attached. Nancy was best kept at a distance. The Brady family's lives were complicated enough right now. Cate knew they didn't need anything further.

Al saw the look on Cate's face and, mercifully, stepped in.

"Aaron, that sounds like a great idea, but unfortunately, I have to get back to work in Oklahoma right away. Our flight leaves tomorrow. Like your Uncle James said, maybe some other time."

Nancy was stewing. Cate recognized the look on her face. She was like a pressure cooker with intensity increasing by the second. She was about to blow. And in record time, too. It usually took her a few more hours before she reached peak pressure levels.

"Enough!" Nancy exclaimed, slinging her hand down hard on the coffee table and making everyone jump. "You need not talk about me like I'm not here."

"Come on," Al said, leaning forward and placing one hand on his wife's back. "That's not what's happening. Take it easy."

"Yeah?" Nancy replied. "How would you describe it

then? It's obvious Cate doesn't like me. She never has. And now she's turned my grandchildren against me. It's a damn shame."

"Nancy, stop it…" Al pleaded.

"Don't try and stop me," Nancy continued, her face narrowing up into a twisted ball of anger and pain.

"Hey, hey," James interjected, raising an arm and reaching out for his sister from across the room. He was protective of her and it showed. Cate appreciated the gesture. "Let's not get carried away. This isn't the time or the place to rehash old wounds. The kids are listening."

"Good," Nancy said, rearing up in her chair. Cate thought she looked a lot like a snake coiled up and ready to pounce. "Let them listen. They should know the truth. I've been banished from their lives because their mother doesn't like me. That's not right, and it's not fair. I did nothing to her. I've been treated horribly."

Cate stood up and, without saying a word, scooped Niko into her arms. Her mind raced as she thought about how to handle the situation. First, she had to get her kids out of the room. They really didn't need this. She walked over to where Jilly was sitting and placed one hand on her shoulder.

"Come with me, sweet pea," Cate said to her daughter. "Let's go into the kitchen and get plates and cups ready for when the pizza arrives. Aaron, will you help us, please?"

Jilly wanted to get away from the uncomfortable situation, so she hopped up immediately and went to the kitchen as her mother asked. Aaron, however, was feeling protective of his grandmother and didn't want to be sent out of the room like a kid. He felt more grown-up now that his dad was gone. Cate hadn't said it to him, but he had heard somewhere that he should be the man of the house. He was taking his new role seriously.

"I'll stay here," Aaron said to his mom.

"What's wrong, Cate?" Nancy asked with a smirk on her face. "Is he finally too old for you to micromanage and control?"

Cate didn't respond to Nancy's insult. Instead, she gave her son a look that let him know he had better move right away. He responded appropriately, begrudgingly walking into the kitchen to join his sister. Cate followed with Niko and provided instructions for what each of her kids could do to help.

When she returned to the living room, Cate was ready to throw Nancy and Al out of the house. She didn't care how sad or exhausted she was. She would find the strength to rally. She would not let her kids get mixed up in Nancy's dysfunctional drama.

Al looked apologetic, like he wished he could somehow compel Nancy to act right.

"I'm sorry, Cate," Al said. "We don't want to cause any trouble. Especially not today."

Cate nodded and smiled kindly at him. She knew he wasn't to blame. Al truly was a good man.

The camaraderie between Cate and Al only angered Nancy further. She stood up, both arms hanging stiff at her sides. She furrowed her brow and narrowed her eyes so much that Cate thought the old woman could hardly see while wearing the expression. Nancy's wrinkled skin turned red as the blood pumped along with the anger.

"I will tell them, Al," she said to her husband, fuming.

Al stood up and stepped close near Nancy's side. He placed his hand on her back again. He was trying to anchor her. Trying to give her a reason to slow down and think things through before she spoke.

"I'm serious, Al," Nancy confirmed. "Don't stop me. This woman needs to know the truth about her sham of a picture-perfect life. She's so smug and self-righteous. It's time I put an end to that."

Al shook his head. It seemed he felt powerless to do anything. Perhaps he was.

Cate didn't appreciate being talked about in this way. She thought everything Nancy was saying was nonsense. She was ready to open her mouth and tell Nancy to leave when her mother-in-law spoke words that would change her life.

Nancy turned, facing Cate. She put her hands on her hips and leaned back, a cool smile covering her face.

"Didn't Mick tell you?" Nancy began.

"Tell me what?" Cate said, responding to Nancy's baiting for the first time.

Nancy chuckled. "Where do you think he got the money to start his business and to pay for this house?"

Cate couldn't hide the look of shock on her face.

"What?" Nancy continued. "You thought a naval officer earned enough to pay for all of this? If you did, you were sorely mistaken."

"Nancy, please…" Al implored.

"That money came from me," Nancy said, satisfied with herself. "I have the promissory notes to prove it. I did my son a favor. And I think I just might call it in and request immediate repayment. My son isn't here to benefit from the money I loaned him anymore. Why should you keep it?"

"What are you talking about?" Cate asked. "Mick told me an investor gave him the money to start his business. Are you saying…?"

"That's right," Nancy said, looking pleased with herself. "It was yours truly."

Cate reached out a hand and grabbed the back of the sofa to steady herself. Dozens of thoughts began swimming through her mind, most of all, she began to fear that she and her children might be placed in a predicament in which they were either beholden to Nancy and subject to her whims or they would have to move out of their home and give up the lifestyle they had become accustomed to. She wondered how Mick could do this to her. She wondered why he hadn't told her the truth.

"I was not aware of this," Cate managed.

"Oh, I know you weren't," Nancy continued.

"But," Cate continued. "We bought this house with our savings. The down payment was made out of our joint checking account. I was there. I saw it for myself."

"Nancy," Al tried again. "You've done enough. Let it rest, I beg you."

"You really are clueless, aren't you?" Nancy asked. "I don't know exactly how, but Mick got involved in something and lost your money. He came to me with his tail between his legs and asked me to replace it. The debt is to me."

James began to get angry. He stood up and walked near his sister, then put one arm around her. "Look," he said. "I don't know what you're talking about, but I know this isn't the time. Truly, Nancy, it isn't the time. We had better call it a night. Where are you two staying? Can I see you back to your hotel?"

Cate was glad James said it so she didn't have to. This day needed to end. She needed time to absorb this new unexpected shock on the heels of the unexpected shock of her husband's death. She didn't know where to begin, but she knew that Nancy needed to leave immediately.

"Yes, goodnight, Al and Nancy," Cate said. She could hear in her own voice that she sounded cold and unemotional. It was all she could manage. She smiled her best phony smile, then turned and walked into the kitchen to join her kids as James ushered her in-laws out the front door. She didn't care if they thought her impolite.

As Cate sat down at the kitchen table, the sun had set and the last glimmer of daylight was lingering low in the sky. She was relieved to be in a room alone with just her kids. And she was relieved that her brother was stepping in to take care of her. She could finally breathe easy for a minute. After all, minute to minute was as much as she could focus on making it through.

Suddenly, there was a loud banging from the back porch as two metal trash cans fell and rolled around. It sounded like too much noise to have been an animal. It sounded like a person was out there. Meesha heard it, too. She ran to the back door, placing her front paws up so she could stand and look out the window. The dog began to bark furiously.

"Mommy, I'm scared," Jilly said as she raced to her

mother's side and wrapped her arms tightly around her waist.

"Me, too," Niko echoed, running to Cate's other side.

Cate looked at Aaron and made eye contact. They both knew that the sound they heard was too big to have been an animal, but they silently agreed to not let the littler kids in on that reality.

"Don't worry," Cate said, wrapping her arms around her youngest children. "We have raccoons sometimes. And there are stray cats in the neighborhood. It was probably one or the other climbing on top of the trash cans and trying to get an evening meal. It's nothing to be concerned about."

"Yeah," Aaron said, trying to help out. "No big deal. I agree with Mom."

Again, suddenly, Cate thought she heard footsteps outside. It sounded like someone was running down from the porch and out of the backyard. From the look on Aaron's face, he had heard it, too. He was mature for his age, but he was still just a kid. Cate didn't want to force him into adult responsibilities before he was ready. She didn't want him to have to worry about Nancy or the sounds in the backyard. Getting over his father's death would be quite enough of a task for the boy.

Cate glanced at the lock on the back door. The knob was turned, indicating that the door was, in fact, locked securely. The motion sensor light had turned on, so she decided they were probably safe for now. She decided that her children's peace of mind was more important than alarming them with a dramatic search scene, so she moved on, alerting no one to what might be happening in the backyard. She would tell her brother later, once Nancy was long gone and the kids were in bed.

If Cate was being honest with herself, she was scared, too. But she knew she'd have to get over that. She was the only adult left in the family and she had to be strong for her kids. She'd had plenty of practice during all those months that Mick was away at sea. She thought to herself how much she had become spoiled with him being home every night. The past year had been so much easier than the ones prior. If Mick had still been alive, he would have gone out back and checked on the noise so Cate didn't have to. He'd had a calm, easy-going demeanor that made everyone around him feel secure. It's why he'd made a good officer in the Navy and it's why he'd made a good husband and a good dad.

"Our pizza should be here any minute," Cate said to her kids. "Sit down at the big table in the dining room."

"Are Grandma and Al staying to eat with us?" Aaron asked.

"No, not tonight," Cate said. "Grandma Nancy and Al had to go. Your uncle James is seeing them out."

Aaron sighed with disappointment. Cate felt bad for her son, but she had limited energy to spend on any one thing. There was a lot for her to juggle. She had to sort things out in her own mind before she let her children get entangled.

Nancy and Al left the house. The kids ate their pizza and went to bed. Then Cate, James, and Rebecca had a good conversation before the Tatums headed home for the night.

Cate decided not to share all of her concerns with

Rebecca, so she told her brother only the basics that night. They discussed Nancy and the possibility that what she was saying about Mick having borrowed money was true. But Cate didn't mention the figure in the distance at the cemetery or the banging noise and the footsteps in the backyard. That would have to wait for another day. She figured she'd give her brother a call when he was at work. Maybe the two of them could meet privately and she could tell him everything. Or maybe, she wouldn't tell James anything at all. Maybe she would just forget that these upsetting things had ever happened. Cate liked that idea. She could forget about the figure in the tree line at the cemetery. She could forget about the noise in the footsteps in the backyard. And she could forget about Nancy and her outrageous claims. Wouldn't that be nice?

Finally, Cate climbed into her big bed. She was tired and wanted nothing more than to get a good night's sleep. Meesha climbed onto Mick's side where she usually slept, down by his feet. Even though Cate had a million things to think about, she told herself that she needed rest to handle them properly. Although she awoke frequently and tossed and turned, she got some much-needed sleep.

4

It turned out to be an entire week before Cate returned to work and the kids returned to school. They had underestimated how hard it would be to get back to a new normal. There had been days where they had all gotten dressed and planned to head out the door, but then something would remind them of Mick and their old life and they'd decide they just weren't ready.

Their opinions were divided regarding what to do with Mick's things. Cate had thought about giving his clothes to charity just to get them out of the house and out of sight. It was too painful each time she opened her closet and saw her husband's clothes hanging there, unworn, on the hangers. She had thought she might keep a few special things for herself, like his blue flannel shirt she liked to wear in the winter when it got too cold in the house. Or his soft U.S. Navy sweatshirt she sometimes threw on to run errands around town on a Saturday morning. She had figured she would keep some things for the kids, too. But she could pack those away or move them to their rooms.

She felt like she had to do *something* to keep from becoming overwhelmed with sadness every time she walked into her dressing room and closet.

Aaron didn't want to give anything up. He wanted to keep his father's closet exactly as it was. Maybe he was in denial about his dad being gone. Maybe, by keeping Mick's closet exactly as it was the morning he left it, Aaron could feel like his father would return someday. Cate understood, but she wasn't sure it was healthy.

Niko was too young to have a strong opinion, but he tended to agree with Aaron. He wanted everything left alone. He just wanted his daddy to come back home.

Jilly, ever the creative child, had other ideas. She'd heard a story at school about a lady in town who made quilts out of special fabric. Jilly desperately wanted some of Mick's clothes to be used that way. Cate thought it was a good idea. At least it would get the items moved and transitioned into a form from which they could be better appreciated and utilized.

But all of those concerns and plans could wait, because, on this day, Cate and her kids were finally going back to work and school. They had discussed it and come up with a new routine. Although Jilly and Aaron used to ride to school with their dad, they agreed that the best thing to do now would be to take the bus. The bus stop was only a few houses down from theirs and some of their friends rode every day, so the plan made sense. Niko's preschool was on the way to Cate's office, so she decided to continue dropping him off and picking him up like before. Ellen and Ron had offered to help with the kids' logistics, but Cate thought it best if she handled things on her own. She didn't want to become overly dependent on her extended family. She was a capable adult. She figured she had better act like one. She knew that her kids were watching her every move.

The leaves had begun to change and their golden hues sparkled in the sun on this cool autumn morning. Jilly and Aaron seemed a little nervous about their new bus ride, but they wanted to do their part to help their mom. They put on their best game faces as they walked out the front door. Cate kissed her children's cheeks and hugged their necks, then they walked purposefully down the front steps, over the driveway, and along the sidewalk up the hill to wait at the bus stop.

Cate finished feeding Niko his breakfast, then helped him wash his face, brush his teeth, and comb his hair. The pair climbed into Cate's SUV and backed out of the driveway, leaving Mick's vehicle parked inside. It felt to Cate very strange to be going back to work when Mick was no longer in the world. It felt like a betrayal to get dressed up and head to the office when Mick's clothes sat unused on hangers in the closet and his vehicle sat unused in the family's garage. But Cate knew she had to move forward. If not for herself, she needed to do it for the kids. She took a deep breath, closed the garage door, and backed out onto the street. She dropped Niko off at preschool without incident and headed into work.

Her workday began just like any other. The building that housed Vine Country Magazine headquarters was in a historic part of downtown that looked like something you'd see in a TV-movie. There were rows of brick buildings with cobblestone paths out front and ivy meandering up the sides. Business owners had revitalized much of the town, and this particular area had become a hotspot for young professionals and hip foodies. Cate liked working in this environment. It felt fun and a little swanky. Tourists often stopped on trips to visit the wineries. Out of towners especially loved to eat at the little downtown restaurants and even took cooking classes offered by local chefs. Being back in the area after her time spent mourning her husband felt good to Cate. It was a needed distraction from the shambles her life threatened to become.

Cate parked her SUV and got out, appreciating the warm sun on her face and the smell of freshly baked bread coming from an establishment nearby. She began the day with a stop at Brick House Cafe to pick up a breakfast sandwich and a cup of coffee. Just like usual, she purchased one for herself and one for Pal, a homeless man who hung around downtown. She'd been buying Pal breakfast sandwiches for months now. In fact, he had probably wondered where she was this past week. Cate hoped he hadn't gone hungry. Like Mick, Pal was a veteran of the U.S. Navy. He was suffering from PTSD and had gotten down on his luck in his old age. Cate felt a soft spot for him and wanted to do her part to help him out.

As Cate exited the café and turned north to head towards her building, to her relief, there was Pal, sitting on a bench and smiling at her. He was a sight for sore eyes.

"Pal!" Cate said, happy to see him. "I have you your sandwich and your coffee. I hope you haven't missed me too much. I had a personal matter come up unexpectedly."

Pal nodded and took the food from Cate's hands. He held up his coffee cup and tipped it towards her as a gesture of thanks.

"I heard what happened to you," he said. "I'm sorry." He mumbled the words as he hastily chewed the sandwich. Cate could tell he was starving.

"Oh?" Cate asked. "What did you hear?"

"Your husband... I heard he was killed. That's terrible. He was a nice man."

Pal had met Mick a few times when he had come by Cate's office to meet her for lunch.

"Yes, thank you," Cate replied, choking back tears. The tears had caught her off guard. She hadn't realized the mention of her husband's name would still cause such an emotional response, here, a full week later.

"I heard he had a proper military funeral, though. Good on him," Pal said as he sloshed the coffee around in his cup, too thirsty to wait for it to cool.

"He did." Cate wondered how Pal knew about the funeral. She couldn't imagine who would have told him. The funeral home and the cemetery are far enough from downtown that he wouldn't have been able to walk there and see for himself. Someone had to have told him. But who?

"It's just a shame how it happened," Pal said. "A real shame."

Cate wasn't clear on the particulars of how it had happened. She was beginning to feel uncomfortable. She had always tried to be friendly to Pal, but she didn't like him knowing intimate details about her husband's death. Particularly not details that she wasn't aware of.

"How do you know about this?" Cate asked pointedly.

Pal was finishing his breakfast sandwich now. He wiped crumbs off the corners of his mouth with one glove, still holding the coffee cup in the other. His hand was shaking and Cate wondered if he might be drunk or drugged. It wouldn't surprise her if Pal had a substance-abuse problem. She had never spoken to him long enough to know if he did. Her skin was beginning to crawl, and she had an uneasy feeling she couldn't explain. It wasn't just Pal. Cate suddenly felt like all eyes were on her. She wondered if she was being watched.

"Word gets around when something like this happens," Pal said.

"Something like what?" Cate asked, beginning to get agitated.

"Like, you know… "

It felt like he was taunting her. Cate began to get frustrated. She wanted to know what Pal knew and where he had heard it. Her body tensed. She began to lean forward as she thought about grabbing the collar of Pal's wrinkled shirt. She thought about giving him a good shake and forcing him to tell her what he knew. He was old and frail. Cate knew she was stronger than he was. If she grabbed him, he wouldn't be able to overpower her or gain the upper hand.

Before she could make a move, Cate felt a soft hand on her shoulder. She jumped, startled by the unexpected touch. Her pulse quickened as she slowly turned to see who was there. It was Sasha Lansing, her friend and colleague. Cate was relieved to see Sasha's friendly face and she let out a burst of air she had been holding.

"Sasha," Cate said.

"Hey, Cate," Sasha said cautiously. "What's happening here?" Sasha looked back-and-forth between Pal, who had started mumbling incoherently, and Cate. "Who is this gentleman?"

Cate couldn't quite remember whether she had ever told Sasha about her daily habit of buying a breakfast sandwich for Pal.

"This is Pal," Cate said. "He's a Navy veteran like Mick was. He got down on his luck and ended up here. For the past few months, I buy myself a breakfast sandwich and a coffee and I buy a second set to give to Pal. It's no big deal."

Sasha raised her perfectly manicured eyebrows. She was a pretty woman in her mid-thirties. She had thick black hair that danced around her shoulders. She was a natural beauty. She didn't have to try very hard, but everything she did to enhance her appearance made a big impact. On this day, she was dressed in a pair of fitted black pants and leather boots that came to her knees. She wore a billowy, long-sleeve blouse with a decorative loose tie around the neck. Cate thought she looked like she could be a real model. She wondered why Sasha hadn't graced the pages of Vine Country Magazine yet. She had the right look which would represent the town of Rosemary Run well. She would probably entice more tourists to visit. Cate thought perhaps she could use an image of her friend paired with an upcoming article.

It surprised Cate that her thoughts could turn so

quickly from grabbing a homeless man and shaking him to which image of her friend might pair well with an upcoming article.

Sasha hesitated before she spoke.

"That sounds lovely," Cate's colleague said. "But when I walked up, it looked like something else was going on. Were the two of you having a disagreement?"

"Gosh, no," Cate said, doing her best to sound calm and collected. "Pal was just telling me he was sorry about what happened. You know, about Mick. Somehow, he heard."

Sasha looked skeptically at her friend, then back at Pal, who rocked back-and-forth and nodded while continuing to mumble. He appeared to be out of it. Cate wondered if it was an act.

"Are you sure?" Sasha asked. "Because it looked like more heated than what you describe."

Sasha bit her lower lip and tilted her head to one side. She was thinking.

"I'm sure," Cate said, taking one of her friend's arms and ushering her away from Pal and the park bench. "It's no big deal, really. Let's head into the office. I'm eager to get back to work."

At first, Sasha stood stiff and remained in place, resisting Cate's attempts to move her. She quickly acquiesced though, giving a final glance at Pal and then walking alongside her friend. Though Cate thought something felt different between them. Sasha was suspicious of her. In all the years they'd been friends, that had never happened before. Cate didn't like it. She wasn't sure what had changed.

The two friends walked arm in arm down the block to the building which housed the magazine headquarters. The hand-carved wooden sign hanging out front was a welcome sight for Cate, who was beginning to realize that she craved familiarity. The pair turned, each placing a hand on the knob of one of the glass doors in the entryway. They stepped inside together, in sync, saying hello to Anna Isley, the young receptionist. The lobby was full, brimming with people. Some, Cate knew. Others, she didn't. Cate still felt uncomfortable as if she were being watched, but she chalked that up to the fact that she was seeing people for the first time since her husband had died. They were probably curious to know how she was doing. Or maybe they didn't know what to say and we're afraid they'd choose the wrong thing and upset her.

Cate couldn't wait to get upstairs and into her private office, away from prying eyes. She wanted to see everyone and to catch up on what she had missed, but she wanted to do it on her own terms without being overwhelmed. In fact, she had already planned the day out in her mind. She would begin by reading the emails she had missed during her week away. She'd turn the monitor on her computer towards the window so she'd have a view of the hills behind the buildings across the street. She loved the fall foliage and thought the display of color would help lift her spirits. Not to mention, she hoped the beautiful scenery might help her forget about the growing list of things she was trying to avoid.

As she walked past the reception desk on her way to the elevators, Anna stopped her.

Oh, no, Cate thought.

She expected the girl to say something awkward about how she was sorry for Cate's loss. Cate appreciated the sentiment, but wasn't in the mood. She figured someone so young couldn't possibly understand what it was like to lose a husband who you've built a life with. She looked at Anna, politely awaiting whatever she needed to tell her.

"Cate, welcome back," Anna said with a smile. She sounded hesitant.

"Thank you," Cate said with as much sincerity as she could muster. She turned back towards the elevators where Sasha had gone ahead of her and began to walk on.

"Wait," Anna said. "There's something else."

Cate winced, then turned around to face the reception desk once more. She was as ready as she could be for more awkward condolences.

"There is an investigator from the local police department here to see you. Detective Fredericks. He's sitting right over there," Anna said, motioning to a front corner of the room.

5

C ate's heart sank. Her first thought was that something must have happened to one of the kids. Maybe Jilly or Aaron on the bus.

"Is everything okay?" she asked Anna, desperately. She knew she had gone from zero to high alarm too quickly. She couldn't help it. Not after what she had been through. "Are my kids okay? Did the bus get into an accident?"

"I think they're fine," Anna said reassuringly, taking Cate's hand in her own. It was a kind gesture, one that surprised Cate. She wouldn't have expected it from someone so young. The thought crossed her mind that maybe she had misjudged Anna. "If he were here to inform you about an accident, I'm pretty sure he'd be wearing a uniform," she said. "This man is dressed in a suit."

Anna was in her early twenties. She'd started at the magazine as an unpaid intern last summer right after she graduated from a design college in San Francisco, but when a full-time receptionist job came open, she took it.

Anna had met and fell in love with a young man from the
area and she wanted to stay in Rosemary Run to see how
things turned out between them. Even though she was
over-qualified to be a receptionist and was better suited to
creating content for the fashion pages, she figured it was a
good start and that she'd be able to move up in the
company when there was an opportunity. Anna had come
from a posh upbringing on Long Island, but she wasn't
conceited. She seemed to have a good head on her
shoulders, which was, no doubt, a credit to solid
parenting.

Cate took a deep breath and pushed her hair behind
one ear. She often played with her hair when she was
nervous. It was a self-soothing move. And it worked. She
collected herself, at least enough to speak to the detective
and to find out what he wanted with her.

"Anna, dear," Cate began. "You're very kind. My
nerves are frazzled these days. But your steady presence
helped me snap back into my right mind. Thank you for
that."

"It's my pleasure," Anna replied. "Anything I can do
to help."

"Would you mind letting Sasha know I'll be delayed
coming upstairs?" Cate said as she motioned her head
towards her friend, who was waiting down the hall in front
of the elevators.

"Of course. I'm on it," Anna said. She really did seem
to want to help. She stepped around the receptionist desk
and headed towards Sasha.

Cate turned the other way and steeled herself as she
approached Detective Fredericks. She didn't know him

well, but she had met Neil Fredericks before. In a town as small as Rosemary Run, you knew everyone on the force. Especially when your brother was a police officer. Besides, Neil was tall and handsome. He wasn't the kind of man Cate could easily forget. He was a few years older than her. About James' age. Neil didn't grow up in Rosemary Run, but he had moved to town not long after Cate had left. From what she understood, he was a good cop and a good guy. He treated people well. He was reasonable. And fair.

Neil stood when he saw Cate coming and he straightened his belt. Cate noticed the handgun fastened securely in its holster at his side. She was used to seeing her brother in his uniform, but James usually left his gun in the car when he came to see her and the kids. The weapon felt dangerous on Neil now. Beads of perspiration collected around her temples. The weather outside was cool, and the lobby was a comfortable temperature. She was sweating because she was nervous.

"Hello, Cate," Neil said as he reached his hand out to shake hers.

"Hello to you, too," she replied. "Neil, right?" She was being coy. She knew his name.

"You remembered!" he said.

"I did."

She didn't mention that his good looks would have been impossible to forget. Come to think of it, he looked quite a lot like her Mick. If she had a type, Neil would be it. Cate felt a pang of guilt thinking about another man this way. She was nowhere near ready to think about dating. She didn't know if she ever would be. But then again, she found herself wondering if Neil was single.

"Is there someplace private we can talk?" Neil asked.

"Sure," Cate said. "I've been out of work for the past week. This is my first day back. I need to check with my boss and let her know where I am. Can you wait for me a few minutes?"

"No worries," Neil said. "I'm sorry for the inconvenience on your first day back to work. I would have come to your house, but I didn't want to scare your kids."

"I appreciate that," Cate said. "They've been through enough. Give me a minute. I'll be right back."

"I'll be here," Neil replied.

Cate left the lobby and went directly to the women's restroom on the other side of the reception desk. She texted her boss, Laura Keller, to let her know that she'd be late getting to her desk. Then Cate stood in front of the mirror and contemplated whether or not she should freshen up her makeup. It was silly. Her emotions were all over the place. But something made her decide that looking her best was important. She applied a fresh coat of red lipstick and powdered her nose. When she received a text back from Laura confirming receipt of her message, she returned to the lobby to face Neil again. She was ready to find out what he was there to tell her. By this time, she figured it was nothing serious. If the matter had been urgent, Neil would have told her right away. His tone was casual and friendly.

When she reached the area where Neil was waiting, Cate found that a second officer was there, too. This one, she definitely knew. It was James. He had his hands on his hips and he was talking to Neil with a look of concern. He stopped and tried to act casual once he saw his sister approaching.

"What are you doing here, big brother?" Cate asked as she hugged James from the side.

"I was just passing by and saw Neil's patrol car, so thought I'd stop in and see what he was up to." James narrowed his eyes at Neil, as if there was more to the story.

"And you found me," Neil said, sounding somewhat irritated. Cate got the idea that James and Neil were at odds about something.

"We can use the conference room right over there," Cate said, pointing. "Will you be joining us, James?"

James rumpled his lips and stared off to one side for a moment.

"You know what? That's alright," he said, looking at Neil. "I'll leave Detective Fredericks to it."

James hugged his sister again and walked out the front of the building. Once he was gone, Neil followed Cate into a conference room and shut the door. They sat down beside each other at a large round table. Cate felt small in the big room with its big table. Having Neil sitting beside her helped. When they were situated she turned towards him, waiting to hear what he had to say.

"What do I owe the pleasure of this visit?" Cate asked. Anna had successfully eased her fears about something being wrong with the kids. Cate didn't know what she was about to hear, but she didn't think it would be anything serious.

"I have a few questions for you, that's all," Neil said. His voice was low and smooth.

"Okay, shoot," Cate said, laughing at the pun as it came out of her mouth. "I don't mean, actually…"

"I know," Neil said. He laced his fingers together on his lap in front of him and began to get down to business. "Mrs. Brady…"

"Please, call me Cate."

"Alright, Cate. I'd like to ask you some questions about your husband Mick in the weeks and months leading up to his death. I'm sure it's a difficult subject, but we've opened an investigation and it's important that you share everything you know with us."

"Okay," Cate said, puzzled. "What kind of investigation? James didn't tell me anything about an investigation."

Neil paused, taking in the fact that James hadn't shared this information with his sister.

"Right now we're in the early stages of gathering evidence for what might soon become a murder investigation."

"What?" Cate asked in disbelief. She didn't mention that the thought had already crossed her mind. "I thought my husband had an accident. Granted, I don't know the details of that accident, but I didn't think it involved foul play."

"And we're not sure either," Neil said as reassuringly as he could. "But it's our job to turn over every stone and to investigate. I assume if someone killed your husband, you would want the responsible parties brought to justice."

"Certainly," Cate said. Her mind was reeling. If they

were opening a murder investigation, why were they talking to her? What did they think she could do to help? She shuddered to think the police might suspect she had something to do with it. An anxious heat flared under her skin, flushed her cheeks. Neil noticed, too. In fact, it seemed like he was watching her for a physical reaction. Cate knew from watching police dramas on TV that the human body will often betray someone who is trying to keep a secret. She wondered if she could count on her body to keep her secrets.

In her calmest, most centered voice, she asked the questions she really needed to know the answers to. "Neil," she began, leaning forward. "Why are you here telling this to me? Is there something specific I can help you with? Because I don't know any more about my husband's death beyond what we've already discussed. James showed up at my door and told me there had been an accident. Then the medical examiner told me Mick's body had been too mangled and that I probably wouldn't want to see it. I don't even know exactly how he died."

"I understand," Neil said. "And forgive me, but I have to ask."

Cate gripped the arms of her chair and braced herself for what she knew was coming.

"Where were you on the night your husband was killed?"

The words rolled off of Neil's tongue as if he'd said them a thousand times. For all Cate knew, maybe he had. This was just another day's work for him. For Cate, however, the question threatened to upend her entire life. Her insides felt like they had suddenly turned to goo as she contemplated the possibility of having Mick's murder pinned on her. She thought about Aaron and his fledgling confidence as a young man. She thought about sweet Jilly and her introverted disdain for things that didn't go her way. And she thought about her baby, Niko, and his fragile boyhood. They needed her as much as she needed them. Mick would never want his children's mother taken away.

Cate hesitated before she answered the question. "Neil, should I hire an attorney? I sort of feel like I should have an attorney here for this conversation."

"Well," Neil replied, leaning back in his chair and keeping both hands out in front of him. "If you think you should, then by all means. That's your right. But I have to tell you, I wasn't expecting that reaction. I envisioned this more like a friendly chat. Do you have something to hide, Mrs. Brady?"

Cate didn't like the way he was suddenly using her last name to address her again. She liked it much better when he called her Cate.

"No, of course not," she said nervously. "Let's back up. No need for this conversation to get heated. On the night my husband was killed, I was at home with all three of our kids. We made homemade pizzas together, and we were cleaning up after dinner when James knocked on the door to tell me the bad news."

Neil pulled out a notepad and a pen from the breast pocket of his uniform and began writing.

"What time did you arrive at your house that evening?"

"I'm not exactly sure," Cate said. "I usually leave the office around four o'clock, and then if Mick hasn't already picked the kids up, I do it. On that day, my oldest children, Aaron and Jilly, had ridden home with friends from the neighborhood. I had tried to call Mick in the early afternoon to see if he could pick up our youngest son, Niko, from preschool. When I didn't get an answer, I assumed my husband was tied up with something and so I picked Niko up myself. I don't know exactly what time we arrived home. Probably somewhere around five."

Cate hoped that Neil wasn't looking for anything more specific. The fact of the matter was she couldn't tell him anymore because she didn't remember. That entire day had become a blur in her mind. It was as if a deep part of Cate's consciousness had blocked it out to protect her from the horrors that unfolded.

"Did you stop anywhere in between picking Niko up from preschool and arriving at your house?"

Cate's heartbeat quickened. She could feel herself beginning to perspire again.

"No, I don't believe so," she said. She could tell that Neil didn't think what she was saying was entirely true.

"Mrs. Brady," he continued. There it was again. Cate didn't like him being so damn formal. "Were you aware of anyone who might have wanted your husband dead?"

It was a reasonable question and one that Cate had immediately thought about herself. For the better part of their marriage, Mick had been secretive about certain things. It had bothered her when she felt like there were events she didn't know about, but he was such a good husband and father that she had overlooked it. Her deepest fear had been that her husband was hiding something from her. Something terrible.

"No, not at all," Cate said. She hoped she sounded convincing.

"Was there anyone he disagreed with? Anyone to whom he owed money?"

Cate immediately thought of Nancy. She wondered whether her mother-in-law could have been in touch with the police. Would she do that? Did Nancy have it in her to try and get Cate in trouble with the law?

"Did my mother-in-law call you?"

Neil narrowed his eyes and took a long, slow look at Cate. "Why would you ask me that?"

"She has it out for me," Cate explained. "I don't know why, but the woman has never liked me. After the funeral last week, she was at our house making comments about how I couldn't afford it without Mick's income."

Cate's face wrinkled as she talked about her mother-in-law. She could feel it.

"Can you afford the house without your husband's income?" Neil asked.

"To be completely honest, I'm not sure yet," Cate said.

"Did your husband have a life insurance policy?"

"Exactly what are you suggesting, Detective Fredericks?" Cate asked. She was the one using last names now. "I'm not sure where this is going. I hope you don't think I had something to do with my husband's death, because I most certainly did not. That's all the time I have for today. As I mentioned, it's my first day back and I need to get to work."

Cate stood up from her chair and reached one hand out to shake Neil's. It was a move that forced him to stand

and respond. Cate hoped it would force him to leave her alone. At least for now.

"Alright then," Neil said agreeably. "Thank you for your time. I'll be back in touch if I have any other questions. And of course, reach out to me if you think of anything that might be helpful. Anything at all."

Neil gave her one of his business cards, then showed himself out of the building. Cate went back into the restroom and enclosed herself in one of the empty stalls. For the first time since Mick's death, she sobbed uncontrollably. It was more than just the gentle crying she'd done at home. All the fear, frustration, and hurt that had been building up inside of her came pouring out all at once. Her shoulders raised and lowered as her chest heaved. Tears streamed down her face as if they were coming from a water spigot that would not turn off. Her eyes burned as she tried in vain to hold the liquid in until, finally, she had exhausted herself enough to settle down. She leaned back hard on one wall of the stall and asked herself a simple question. *Why me?*

6

D etective Fredericks knew something wasn't right when he left his interview with Cate Brady at Vine Country Magazine. He had been at this long enough to tell when people weren't telling the truth. He knew that even if Cate wasn't lying outright, there was something significant that she was holding back. Rosemary Run was a sleepy little town that didn't see much action, and this case was exciting him. The thought of him having a chance to investigate and solve a murder made him happy.

He liked Cate Brady, and he found her very attractive. So attractive, in fact, that if she weren't a grieving widow, he would ask her out. He had been single for far too long and Cate was just the kind of woman he had hoped to settle down with. But Neil Fredericks was a man of the law. He would bring anyone guilty to justice. Even Cate Brady.

Neil climbed into his car and drove the two miles back to the police station, which was situated on a hill overlooking the valley. He glanced at the downtown in the distance as he stepped out of his vehicle and continued to think about Cate. He was making a mental to-do list of things to check into. He was eager to make notes and add to his growing file.

When he walked into the station and sat down at his desk, he found that he had received two messages that morning while he had been away.

The first was from a colleague of Cate's at Vine Country Magazine named Sasha Lansing. She had called in to report an altercation between Cate and a homeless man named Pal, which she had seen take place this morning. Sasha had overheard the two of them discussing Mick's death. She claimed that Cate had acted strangely when she approached. Sasha made it clear she didn't know much and didn't want to get Cate into any trouble, but that she thought she should make a report, just in case.

The second message was from a woman named Nancy DeAngelo, Cate's mother-in-law. She wouldn't tell the officer who took the call any details, but said she was in town from Oklahoma and wanted to speak with Detective Fredericks right away.

7

The rest of Cate's workday was uneventful. She worked through lunch and kept her head down to take her mind off her troubles. There was plenty to catch up on and she had deadlines to meet, so staying distracted came easy. Few people walked by her office all day and even fewer stopped to talk. Maybe they were remaining at a distance on purpose. Or maybe, it was just a coincidence and they hadn't had reason to walk by that day. Cate didn't much care either way. Her life had become complicated enough. She wanted to keep things simple.

When four o'clock arrived, Cate closed up her computer and headed out to pick Niko up from preschool. Aaron and Jilly had already texted to let her know they'd made it home safely thanks to the school bus.

Cate hoped the evening could be low key. Her head hurt from crying and she needed some downtime to think. There were still several casseroles in the freezer which friends and neighbors had made and dropped off after Mick died. Cate planned to pop one in the oven, eat with the kids, and then crawl into bed. She thought maybe she'd watch a little TV or read more of the novel which she had been in the middle of back before her world got turned upside down. She continued to crave routine and normalcy. Besides, the many problems that were stacking up in her life did not have easy answers. She felt helpless to do much about any of them.

On the way to Niko's school, rain plummeted down so hard and so fast that Cate thought the entire sky had opened up. It was getting dark earlier and earlier as the October days reached towards November. The additional dark clouds from this evening's storm only enhanced the gloomy mood. Traffic was thick and came to a stop several times as the town's people headed home for the evening. Tourists on foot bobbed and weaved through the lines of vehicles trying to get out of the rain.

The air was cool outside. It wasn't nearly as cold as it had been on the day of Mick's funeral, but the warm days of summer had come and gone. Cate turned the heater on in her SUV so it would be warm when Niko got in. She knew he didn't like wearing his coat underneath his seatbelt. Cate didn't blame him. She didn't much like wearing hers that way either.

She thought back to living in Connecticut when it got so cold in the winter that you had to bundle up to go outside, even for short periods. Cate preferred life in Rosemary Run where it got cold, but rarely too cold. A sweater or a light coat was all you needed, most winters. Especially if you dressed in layers. On days when a light coat alone wasn't enough, a coat and a sweater together would usually do the trick. Cate liked the way the valley got cold enough for there to be a change of seasons, but not so cold that its residents had to become shut-ins with piled up snow which prevented people from getting around town.

When Cate arrived at Niko's school, she parked her car along the curb out front and held her purple umbrella as she walked inside to sign her boy out. His teachers said he had done well on his first day back. Cate was relieved to hear that her son had gotten through the school day successfully. She had been afraid that it would be too much. Or too fast.

As the two of them returned to their vehicle, Cate noticed a dark-colored sedan with its lights on idling at the back of the parking lot. Something about it caused the hairs on the back of her neck to stand up. There were few other cars in the parking lot, which made it odd that this one was so far in the back. Especially given the rain. If it was a parent here to pick their child up, Cate couldn't think of any reason they would wait so far away from the front entrance. The more she thought about it, she remembered that there had been a dark-colored sedan in traffic behind her ever since she had left the parking garage near her office. If she was being followed, the fact that this person now knew where her son went to school unnerved her completely. It was one thing to have someone tangle with her, but she drew the line where her kids were concerned.

She tried to talk herself out of being alarmed. She figured maybe the grief was getting to her. But she couldn't shake the feeling that she was being watched.

Cate hastily helped her son into his booster seat and

closed his door. She hurried around the vehicle and got in the driver seat, careful to not let the umbrella block her line of sight. She put the umbrella down on the floorboard, closed and locked her door, and sped away.

Cate knew she was driving too fast for the weather, but she needed to lose the car she was now certain was following her. She decided not to go directly home for fear that the person in the car would learn where she lived. Instead, she headed out of town towards the bay, following a road that climbed in elevation and ran along the edge of the ridge, high above downtown. She purposefully headed in the opposite direction of her neighborhood to throw off the person tailing her.

She considered calling Neil Fredericks to report that she was being followed. It would be easier to call him than her brother. James was sure to get worked up at any mention of his little sister being in danger. Besides, it might help her standing with Neil if he had some sympathy for what she was going through. Using one hand, she rifled through her purse and pulled out Neil's business card. Then, carefully, she dialed the numbers to his mobile phone, one by one. He picked up on the first ring.

"Hello?" His voice was as smooth on the telephone as it had been in person. For a few seconds, Cate forgot about the dangers she might be in and became mesmerized by Neil's voice.

What a catch he was.

"Um, yes," she said, snapping out of it. "Neil?"

"Is this Cate? Cate Brady?" She thought he sounded like he might be glad to hear from her.

"It is!" she said, focusing again on her current predicament as she continued to speed out of town and towards the bay. Rain was falling even harder now in a torrential downpour. It was hard to see more than a few feet in front of her vehicle. "I'm sorry to bother you this late in the day. I realize you may have left the office already."

"No worries," Neil said. "What can I do for you?"

"I'm driving," Cate began. "I... I know it sounds crazy, but I think I'm being followed. I have my youngest son, Niko, here in the car with me and I'm heading out of town because I don't want the person following me to know where I live. I don't know what else to do. My two older kids are at home by themselves." And then, quietly, "I'm scared."

Neil paused before responding, but only for a minute. "Here's what we will do. I want you to turn around and come back into town. Drive directly to the police station. Don't stop on the way, but slow down for me, please. We don't want you getting in an accident in this rain."

"How did you know I was speeding?"

"I had a hunch."

"Okay," Cate said. "Neil, thank you."

Cate felt safer when she hung up the phone. She felt watched over and protected. She was glad she had reached out to Neil. She slowed down and calmly turned around, heading away from the bay and back towards town. Going to the police station was a perfect solution. Cate wished she had thought of it herself. But then again, it was kind of nice the way Neil had suggested it. If she had thought of it herself and had gone directly there, she wouldn't have had the chance to see how Neil would react to the thought of her in danger.

Still worried about Aaron and Jilly at home alone, Cate called her neighbor, Sean, and asked him to check in on them. If someone was following her, they might already know where she lived. And, although she didn't want to admit it to herself, the footsteps she heard in the backyard the night of Mick's funeral probably meant that whoever was following her already knew where she lived. It made her sick inside. She had been trying to avoid the issue, hoping it would go away. She'd like to think this was all her imagination.

Sean was retired and usually home, so Cate didn't think it would be any trouble for him to pop over to her house. His grandson, Mitchell, was probably home from school already, anyway. Maybe he and Jilly could do homework together. Jilly would find it awkward that she had to hang out with him, but she'd get over it. It was more important that they kept her safe. Having an adult at the house was a necessity if someone tried to bother them. Aaron and Jilly were mature for their ages, but they couldn't be expected to handle a stalker who might want to do them harm.

The call went to Sean's voicemail. Cate didn't leave a message, but he must have recognized her number because he called back within a few minutes. The old man said he was happy to go by her house and would remain there until she and Niko got home. Cate thanked him and felt grateful to have such a good neighbor nearby. She felt like Aaron and Jilly would be safe under Sean's watchful eye.

On the way back into town, Cate debated whether to call James and fill him in. She'd been meaning to talk to him anyway, but she didn't want to alarm him. Especially if she was overreacting. She knew her brother would stand up for her and would stop at nothing to protect her and the kids. She was glad to have him in her corner, yet there was something about that conversation he and Neil were having this morning which made her hesitant to get her brother involved. Cate thought maybe she should just let Neil handle it. She decided to wait and do just that. There were so many questions that were unanswered. She wanted to wait until she got a handle on at least a few of them before sharing what she knew with James.

Cate looked back at her youngest son in the rearview mirror. He was such a good boy. She thought about how much he looked like his dad the way he was sitting with his head leaned over to one side. He was looking out the window, watching the rain. For him, life was simple and easy until the day his father was taken away. Niko's entire world changed that day. Never again would he be able to live completely carefree. In a single afternoon, he had come to understand the cruel reality that life can be harsh and difficult and unforgiving. Cate's heart hurt for her boy. She thought herself a good mom and would have done anything to keep her children from experiencing this pain, including trading places with Mick if that had been an option. Cate Brady would have done anything for her family.

"Mommy?" Niko asked softly.

"Yes, my darling. What is it?" Cate was calmer now. She felt like she could breathe deeply again.

"Where are we going?"

He said it in such a trusting voice. It sounded like it would be have been okay no matter where his mom was taking them.

"We're going to meet a friend of mine named Neil," Cate said, choosing her words carefully. "He's a detective on the local police force."

"Does he wear a uniform and carry a gun?" Niko asked.

"He usually carries a gun, yes," Cate replied. She wondered what her five-year-old knew about guns, anyway. She didn't think they had discussed them much. What he knew must have come from TV and movies. That is unless his older siblings had been talking to him. "But Neil is a detective, so he wears a suit like Daddy. Detectives don't wear uniforms like other police officers."

Cate could see her son tense up at the mention of his daddy. Come to think of it, Niko hadn't talked too much about his father since he died.

"You know," Cate began. "It's okay to talk about Daddy. Just because he's gone doesn't mean we will forget him. We could never do that."

Niko nodded his head, hesitantly. He was quiet for another few moments. Cate didn't break the silence. She wanted to give him space for his thoughts and feelings. When he spoke, Niko wanted to know more about Neil.

"Will he have a badge to prove that he's a police officer?" It was an excellent question. Cate and Mick had always told the kids to look for a police officer if they were ever lost or in trouble, and they had pointed out how it was important to look for the police officer's badge to identify them properly.

"Yes, my sweet boy. He will."

"Are we going to see him at the police station?"

"Yes, that's exactly right. We are. You're my smart boy, Niko Brady," Cate said, trying to sound as normal as possible. Niko smiled, basking in his mom's adoration.

Cate wasn't sure Niko had ever been to a police station. She didn't think he had. She hoped it wouldn't scare him.

8

W hen Cate and her young son arrived at the Rosemary Run police station, the rain was still coming down steadily. Visibility remained low, and it looked like the wet weather would continue for quite some time. Thunder boomed softly in the distance. The air outside felt dangerous.

Cate was unbuckling her seatbelt when Neil appeared beside her vehicle, shielded from the water by a large, black umbrella. His chiseled features and his deep-set blue eyes looked especially handsome in the low light.

"You made it," Neil said, smiling, as Cate rolled down the driver's side window. "You said one of your sons is with you?" Neil leaned forward to glance in the back seat.

"Yes, this is Niko Brady," Cate said as she introduced Neil to her youngest son. Niko waved cheerfully, then Neil did the same.

Cate could tell Neil wanted to talk privately without Niko overhearing, yet he wasn't inviting the two of them into the station. Maybe he didn't want the little boy to get out in the rain.

"Cate, why don't you step outside so we can talk for a few minutes?"

She liked that he was using her first name again. He seemed to have softened since this morning when he was driving a hard line with his probing questions.

"In the rain?"

"You can stand here with me, under my umbrella. It's large enough for both of us."

Cate's pulse quickened at the thought of standing so close to Neil Fredericks. She told herself to stop it. This was not a social call. And besides, her husband had only been dead for little more than a week. Cate told Niko she'd be just outside and to stay buckled in his booster seat, then she climbed out of the SUV and stood next to the handsome detective. She could smell a hint of his aftershave. Perhaps the rain was making the smell more noticeable.

"Are we going inside?" Cate asked, already knowing the answer.

"I thought we'd talk out here, if it's alright with you," Neil replied.

Dynamics between the two of them were changing. Any formality that was present previously was being abandoned. Cate thought perhaps Neil had learned something which had moved him firmly onto her side. Hopefully, this meant he was no longer suspicious of her. Hopefully, he'd stop asking questions about her whereabouts the evening her husband died.

"So, tell me what happened," Neil instructed.

Cate debated whether to tell him the whole story. She quickly decided that she would. She was genuinely concerned for her safety. Especially if Mick's death hadn't been an accident, because whoever killed him could be after her and the kids. She trusted the local police. She trusted Neil.

"It started the day of Mick's funeral," she began. "As the undertakers were lowering his casket into the ground, I jerked and looked away. I hadn't planned to turn my body around, but it was overwhelming to see my husband buried. Everyone else was watching the casket, paying their last respects. When I turned around, I saw someone standing along the tree line at the edge of the cemetery. At first, I wasn't even sure it was a person. All I could make out was a shadowy figure. But as my eyes focused, I could tell more. I don't know whether it was a man or a woman, but the person saw me seeing them and took off running into the woods."

"Huh," Neil said, taking it in.

"And then," Cate continued. "Later that evening, after most of the guests had left our house, I was in the kitchen with the kids when we heard a loud banging sound on the back porch. I could tell our metal trash cans had been knocked over. I first thought there must have been an animal messing around. Like I told the kids that night, we have stray cats in the neighborhood. Cats and raccoons have shown up trying to mess with the trash before. But what I didn't tell my kids is that immediately after the banging sound, I heard what I'm sure were footsteps, running away. I'm certain someone was there."

"Did you go outside and check it out?" Neil asked, the rain still pouring down around them.

"No, I didn't," Cate said. "James and Rebecca were there. I could have asked my brother to check it out. I thought about it, but he was seeing my in-laws out. Nancy and Al had come in town from Oklahoma for the funeral. I wanted to get that woman out of my house as soon as possible, so I didn't want to delay their exit by mentioning the noise to James. Our dog barked. Maybe that helped scare the person off."

Cate noticed that Neil seemed to react when she mentioned her in-laws. He pulled his head ever so slightly back. She wondered what that was about. She liked Neil, and she hoped they could converse without her feeling like he was recording everything she did for his future reference. Cate didn't want to be just another case to him. She wanted to be something more. Friends, perhaps. She thought that would be a good start.

"I'd considered mentioning it to James, but I hadn't had a chance and didn't want to make a big deal out of it," Cate continued. "Truly, I thought maybe it was just the grief getting to me. I've never gone through anything like this before and it's hard to know what's normal and what's not."

Neil's lips moved into a sympathetic frown. He cared about her. Cate could tell. It was hard for her to believe that she had only known Neil as an acquaintance until this morning. It felt like she had known him much longer.

"I can't imagine what you're going through," Neil said kindly. "I've never been married. The closest loss I can compare yours to is when I lost my mom. That was the hardest thing I'd ever had to face. I'll bet losing a spouse is even harder. I'm so sorry."

Cate believed him.

"Thank you," she said. "That's very kind. Most people don't know what to say, so they say something ridiculous. Or nothing at all. But your words are heartfelt. They mean a lot."

She noticed herself leaning a little closer to him.

"So what happened today?" Neil asked. "Have there been any other incidents between the day of the funeral and now?"

Neil didn't tell Cate that he'd spoken with both Sasha and Pal about this morning's incident. Nor did he tell her he'd spoken with Nancy. Little did she know, Cate's case had taken up Neil's entire day.

"No other incidents until now," Cate replied. "I've had a nagging feeling that I was being watched. I chalked that up to what happened at the cemetery and then, you know, later that evening. The kids and I have been mostly holed up at home until this morning when we all went back to work and school."

"And today?" Neil asked again, patiently. He didn't intend to push her. This was a long game. A marathon and not a sprint.

"Today, when I left my office, I noticed a dark-colored sedan following me," Cate continued. "At first, I thought it was my imagination. I've been doubting myself more than usual lately."

"That's understandable," Neil offered.

"But when I walked out of Niko's preschool after signing him out in the office, I saw the same dark-colored sedan in the back of the parking lot. It was just sitting there with its lights on, idling. In the rain. The parking lot was nearly empty. Doesn't that strike you as odd?"

"Maybe so," Neil agreed. "Could you tell the make and model of the car?"

Cate shook her head from side to side. "No, I was focused on getting Niko buckled in and getting out of there."

"Close your eyes for a minute and try to remember," Neil instructed.

"Here?"

"Yes," he said. His voice made Cate feel safe. She glanced at Niko to make sure her little boy was still buckled into his seat, then did as Neil asked. She wrinkled her nose as she closed her eyes tightly, her cheeks feigning a smile.

"Try to relax," Neil instructed. "Go back in your mind and be there."

Cate nodded her head to let him know she was trying.

"Be there," he said again. "What can you tell me about the car you see?"

To Cate's surprise, she could remember it in greater detail. Neil was good at his job. She was impressed.

"It was a newer car," she said. "Maybe brand new. It was either dark, charcoal gray or black. It was hard to tell in the rain."

"Good," Neil said. "How big was the car?"

"Big. I think it would probably be considered a full-size. It looked kind of sporty. It was contoured around the sides and up near the headlights."

"Did it have any markings on it? Like a racing stripe?"

"No, it was definitely plain."

"Nice job," Neil said. "Did you see where the car went when you pulled out of the parking lot?"

Cate opened her eyes. "As I drove away, it did too. Following behind me. I was so freaked out that I just sped ahead, swerving through traffic to try and get away from it. When I looked back, I couldn't see it in my rearview mirror. But in all this rain, it was hard to tell what vehicles were behind me."

"Alright, well, now I have a good idea what to be on the lookout for."

"Do you think we're safe?" Cate asked timidly.

Neil shrugged his shoulders a little, but stopped himself. He could tell Cate was looking to him for reassurance and already, he didn't want to let her down. "Do you have a security system at your house?"

"I believe so," Cate replied. "I don't think it's active, but I'm pretty sure the house is wired for one. Mick handled that kind of thing when we were married." It was the first time Cate had referred to her marriage in past tense. It stung a little.

"How about you begin there?" Neil asked. "I can give you the name of a friend of mine at a local security company. He'll take good care of you. He will make sure that your house is set up on their monitoring service, with both cameras and alarms. That will go a long way. If anyone comes to your back door again, we can take a look at the footage and hopefully identify them."

"Okay," Cate said.

She didn't tell Neil, but she was reluctant to have her house monitored by a security company. She didn't want to live her life in fear and she didn't want her kids to grow up that way either. She thought to herself that she might wait awhile before following Neil's advice. After all, no one had physically threatened them yet. These incidents might just be in her imagination. She had heard how flimsy they were as the words came out of her mouth. The dark-colored car in the school parking lot might have just been leaving at the same time. Maybe she was becoming paranoid. And a security system with cameras would only feed that paranoia.

"I appreciate you coming out here and talking to me like this, what with the rain," Cate said, gesturing up to the sky. "I'll let you get back to whatever you were doing. I should head home and make sure my kids are okay. They'll be wanting supper soon and I always tell Aaron to wait to cook until Mick... Until I'm home." Cate told herself that she needed to stop referring to Mick as if he were still a part of the family.

"It's no problem," Neil said. "I'm happy to help. You have my numbers. I wrote my mobile number on the business card I gave you this morning. Use that to call me directly, anytime. You can text if it's more convenient. Let me know when you're ready for the name of my friend from the alarm company. And I'll let him know you'll be reaching out soon."

"Thank you," Cate said, looking up at Neil and enjoying another whiff of his aftershave. "This has been nice."

"It has," he agreed. "Try to relax, please. Be smart about how you handle yourself and leave the worrying and investigating to me. Deal?"

Cate liked the way he said to leave the worrying to him, but she wasn't so sure about the investigating part. She hoped they could move on from that part soon. She hoped there would be a soon for the two of them.

"Deal," she said, then she smiled at Detective Neil Fredericks politely and climbed back into her SUV.

On the way home Cate thought about how she had been acting like a crazy person, speeding through town in the rain and driving towards the bay while two of her children remained at home alone. Where had she thought she was going, anyway? It had been years since Cate had needed to run away. Even back then, she was running to Mick after a bad breakup with a boyfriend she'd had since high school. Those days had long passed. It was time for Cate to settle down.

9

"I'm gaining her trust," Detective Fredericks said to his partner, Luke Hemming, as he took off his coat and shook it out to get some of the water off. They were playing good cop-bad cop. The time for Luke's bad-cop routine had not yet come. But they both figured it would. It almost always did.

"Does she suspect anything?" Luke asked. "It will make things easier for us if she remains oblivious."

"I don't think so," Neil said. He felt bad. He really liked Cate. But he had a job to do. And he couldn't ignore the growing body of evidence that was stacking up against her.

10

W hen Cate arrived home, she didn't go inside. She didn't have the energy to cook and then clean the mess. Instead, she texted Aaron and Jilly to come out to the SUV. Cate thanked Sean for staying with them as he and Mitchell headed home, then she drove all three of her kids to her parents' house.

Cate had been trying to stay strong and to be independent, but she was tired. She knew her parents would welcome her and her children with open arms if she showed up asking for help. For tonight, she needed help with dinner and didn't want the hassle of a restaurant. Cate feared that at some point soon, she might need Ron and Ellen's help with a lot more than a meal. She pushed those thoughts away as she knocked on the wooden front door of her parents' farmhouse, then used her key to enter. She hadn't told them she was coming. She hadn't needed to.

"Hello, Mom? Dad?" Cate called out, raising her voice more than usual to be heard over the rain.

"Anybody home?" Aaron added.

Jilly held Niko's hand as they walked inside their grandparents' house. The kids felt comfortable there. In some ways, they were more comfortable there than at their own house. They had been coming to Rosemary Run to visit their grandparents long before they moved here and bought a place of their own.

Ron and Ellen's farmhouse sat on a beautiful, ten-acre property just outside of town on Pleasant Valley Road. The home was built in 1905. The couple had moved in a few years before James was born and had begun the renovation process soon after. They had taken the house down to the studs and rebuilt everything from the ground up. They had done much of the work themselves, Ron framing the house and hanging drywall and Ellen painting and landscaping. The result was a work of art which had provided a happy childhood home for James and Cate to grow up in. As an adult, regardless of what had been going on in Cate's life, she knew she could always come home to a safe place where she was loved and accepted unconditionally.

The property featured a pond which the family often canoed on. It also had a small vineyard. Ron and Ellen had tended to the grapes by themselves for many years, but recently hired part-time help as it was becoming too much for them. The same was true with their animals. The Tatums had a quaint little farm going with a couple each of goats, cows, and sheep, plus a rooster, a dozen hens, and an Australian Shepherd named Joey who watched over them all. The animals provided supplementary income for the working-class couple, but mostly, the pair enjoyed farm life. The hired help was only there for a few hours a day, so their presence didn't feel intrusive. Much of the time, when Ron and Ellen weren't at their day jobs, it was just the two of them and their animals. They were both happy that way. The entire property had charm and good energy about it. They had taken to referring to the place as Pleasant Valley Farm and the name fit. Cate was grateful for the respite the little farm provided.

"Hello?" Cate called out again, even louder this time, as she and the kids took off their rain jackets and folded up their umbrellas inside the front room. It was strange for her parents not to answer. Ellen's car and Ron's truck were both parked outside in their usual spots. "They have to be here somewhere," Cate mumbled to herself. "Joey?" she tried. The dog wasn't in the house either.

"Maybe they're out at the barn," Jilly said. "Tending to the animals."

"Ah," Cate said, raising her eyebrows. "I'll bet you're exactly right, Jilly. Good girl. There's probably extra work to do to keep the animals' bedding dry and fresh."

"Should we go out to look for them?" Aaron asked. "I'd like to see the animals."

"Yeah!" Niko said excitedly. "Mommy, I want to see the animals, too."

Cate was glad to see her kids excited for a change, but she didn't like the thought of them getting all muddy and dirty in the barn. It would be a big mess to clean up when they got home.

"Please, Mom?" Aaron said, seeming to know what she was thinking.

As she looked at the faces of her three darling children, all eager with anticipation, she couldn't say no. She knew that animals were good therapy. And her kids needed that.

"You know what?" she began. "Let's go on out. Who cares if we get wet and dirty? Being with the animals for a while might just do us some good."

"Yay!" the kids cheered in unison.

"Thank you, Mommy," Niko said. He was so polite for his age. And so sincere. He melted Cate's heart time after time with his sweet ways. Something about the fact that Cate knew Niko was her last baby meant she had a soft spot for him. She tried to cherish every moment of his childhood.

"You're very welcome," Cate said. "But we won't stay out long because we need to eat dinner. I don't know about you, but I am hungry."

The kids agreed and the four of them put their coats back on and picked up their umbrellas, then walked out the back door. They could see that the light was on in the distance in the barn's direction, so Cate suspected that Jilly had been exactly right. The barn was about a quarter of a mile from the house. It didn't take long to walk there, but they were moving slower than usual tonight.

The rain continued to pour massive amounts of water around them and lightning lit up the sky. It looked to Cate like the storm had been even heavier here at her parents' house than it had in her neighborhood. She and her kids held hands as they stepped over fallen limbs and across big puddles. Even as the storm raged around them, Cate felt safe on her parents' farm. She knew that as soon as she saw their faces, it would help lift her worries away. She was grateful to have such good parents. They were a gift in her life that she made sure to never take for granted.

When they arrived at the barn, sure enough, Ron and Ellen were there, reassuring the frightened farm animals as Joey sat and looked on. He was an intelligent dog. Content to watch everything happening around him.

"Well, hello!" Ron said. "Fancy meeting you here." He laughed at his own greeting. Cate's dad thought himself a comedian.

Ellen waved one hand playfully to shush her husband. "What a nice surprise," she said as she walked over to hug Cate and the kids.

"Hey, Mom and Dad," Cate said. "It's been a long day and I thought I'd stop in to see if we might eat dinner with you. I didn't realize you'd be out here."

"But we're glad you are," Aaron said, attempting to finish his mother's sentence while walking over towards Bella the sheep.

Cate and her parents chuckled at Aaron's enthusiasm. The mood was light, despite the bad weather.

"Say," Ron began, winking at his daughter, then looking at his grandchildren, one by one. "I could use some help to freshen up the goats' bedding. Would anyone like to assist? I know Fred and Ginger would be very appreciative." Ron had named the pair of goats Fred and Ginger after Fred Astaire and Ginger Rogers because he said they had looked like they were always dancing when they were kids. The man got quite a kick out of himself. Cate supposed it was good that he could always keep himself entertained. He usually kept those around him entertained.

"Me!" Niko exclaimed, raising his hand in the air as if he were in a classroom at school.

"Me, too!" Jilly added.

"You've got it," Ron said, motioning for the kids to come over and join him.

"I'll stay here and comfort Bella, if that's alright," Aaron said as lightning flashed outside. "She seems scared."

"That's perfect," Ellen said to her grandson. "Just pet her on the head there and stand close against her side. It will help her feel safe and loved. And while you're at it, please check on her food and water supply to make sure she has enough for the night."

Aaron nodded and smiled. Cate noticed that all three of her kids were loosening up. She hadn't realized they'd been so tense. Meesha had been an important source of comfort for them in the days since their father died, but these farm animals seemed to be making an even bigger impact. Maybe that was because there were so many of them. Or maybe, it was because the kids didn't get to see them every day and they seemed like more of a novelty.

"There's something amazing about hanging around with these animals," Ellen said, noticing the same thing as her daughter. "That's why Ron and I have them in the first place. They keep us sane. I don't know what we'd do without them."

Cate knew that when her Mom's job as a school librarian went on break for the summer, it allowed Ellen to spend a lot more time out here enjoying farm life. This time of the year, though, she had to settle for evenings and weekends.

Lightning strikes were coming closer and happening more often now. The wind was so strong that the rain was blowing sideways. This was turning into the worst storm Rosemary Run had seen in a long time.

"It's getting bad out there," Ron said.

"I see it," Cate said. "But honestly, I'm happier right here and now than I've been since, you know... And I think the kids would say the same."

No one commented, but they sat quietly together, reflecting on the moment. It didn't matter to Cate and her kids that they were in a rainstorm, or that they would leave smelling like farm animals and have to spend time washing themselves and their clothes a while extra when they returned home. It didn't matter that they were hungry for dinner or that it was a school night and they needed to get up early in the morning. The only thing that mattered was that they were enjoying life's simple pleasures as they gathered together and experienced the world in each other's company. Cate thought about how lucky she was for the love she had in her life. Even though her husband was gone, those who remained were some of the best people. She thought that with her family by her side, she could get through any storm-- literal or figurative-- that life might throw her away.

With a loud boom and a crash, a bolt of lightning struck the power lines outside of the barn, knocking them to the ground, sparking and popping, and turning off the lights. Everyone jumped, frightened by the intensity of the storm and the sudden descent into total darkness. Joey barked loudly at the sounds.

"Mommy! I'm scared," Niko said.

"Me too!" Jilly echoed.

It reminded Cate of the night of Mick's funeral when they heard the noise on the back deck, only this threatened to be much worse.

"Jilly, honey, put your arm around your little brother until an adult gets to you," Cate said. "I'm coming."

"Okay," Jilly replied.

Ron had been close to the kids, but had stepped away to look at the damage outside.

"Everybody stay put," Ron instructed, raising his voice to be heard over the storm.

"Okay!" they all called back.

Tools clanked around as Ron searched for a flashlight or a lantern. The animals squirmed and bucked around in their stalls, trying to discharge the fear from their bodies.

"Aaron, stay there. I'm nearby and I'm coming to you," Ellen said.

He shouted his okay.

By the time Cate reached Jilly and Niko, they were both shaking like leaves. She grabbed them and pulled them close, surprised by how quickly things had turned sour.

"It's okay, my darlings," Cate said to her children in the most reassuring voice possible. "It's just a storm. We have shelter and we're going to be alright."

She could feel the kids nod their heads yes as they pressed up against her. They were such kind souls. So trusting. Cate wondered if she should've stayed home tonight rather than having come to her parents. Even though they had just experienced the happiest time since Mick died, Cate feared it had turned on a dime and could become the worst time. She felt the responsibility to her children, and she began to doubt that she was doing her best for them.

"I'm here with Aaron," Ellen called out. "We're okay over here. Bella is, too."

It relieved Cate that her mom was there to comfort her oldest son. Aaron might have acted like he didn't need comforting, but Cate knew he still did.

"Fred and Ginger are okay!" Niko called out in his little voice, trying to help.

"I think I left my flashlight up at the house," Ron said. "The lantern is probably there, too. I need to go up and grab them. Everybody stay here while I go. I'll be back as quickly as I can."

Cate wanted to ask her dad not to go. She was becoming afraid, too, and her mind was swirling with the dangers that might await him out in the storm, especially considering the downed power lines. She couldn't bear the thought of losing another one of her closest family members.

"Why don't you wait with us until the storm calms down a little?" Cate asked her dad. She was impressed that she had sounded so calm and had phrased the question in a reasonable way. Inside, she wanted to yell much more irrational words. Although Cate couldn't explain it, she was getting a sick feeling in the pit of her stomach. The hairs on the back of her neck were standing up again.

"I don't think the storm will slow down for a while," Ron replied. "Don't worry about me. I'll be okay."

"Dad," Cate called out, the fear evident in her voice now. "Wait. Please."

"It's okay, Cate Bear, truly," Ron said. He had called her Cate Bear when she was a kid and still did so every once in a while. Hearing him call her that now both brought Cate comfort and made her more afraid all at once.

It was pitch black. So black, that they couldn't see things even when they were right in front of their faces. Under normal conditions, there were no other lights for nearly a mile. But tonight was impossibly dark. Even the moon and the stars were blocked out by storm clouds.

Cate could hear her dad opening his umbrella and stepping towards the open barn door, which would lead him on the path to the house. She knew he was determined to go, whether she liked it or not. She knew he should go. They needed a source of light to get everyone out safely. But she didn't want him to.

Before Ron could take his first step toward the house, a new bolt of lightning came crashing down and split a large tree just outside of the barn in two. The roof moaned and cracked as half of the tree crashed down into it, creating a large, gaping hole on one side of the structure. The animals went wild with fear now, yelling and thrashing around. The backside of the goats' enclosure had apparently fallen down because they could be heard yelling out in fear as their voices trailed farther and farther into the distance.

Niko began to cry. He couldn't verbalize it quickly

enough, but he heard the goats running away and it terrified him. He twisted at Cate's side and she thought for a moment he might try to run after them. Jilly placed her hands over her ears and pressed her head tightly into the crack of Cate's arm like a little ostrich who was trying to hide from reality.

"Is everyone okay?" Ron called out.

They all answered yes. *Thank God*, Cate thought.

"I have to go to the house," Ron said. "I need light to get everyone out safely and to assess the damage."

"And the goats…" Ellen said, sadly.

"One thing at a time," Ron replied to his wife. "I'm going now. Stay here."

Ron hesitated for a minute as he prepared himself to go out into the nasty weather.

Ellen, Cate, and the kids stood, doing as they were told, staring into the blackness and afraid for their safety. They looked in the direction Ron's voice was coming from because they knew that was the way they'd see him when he returned. They didn't discuss it between them, but they each knew they were watching for him to return with the light. It would be his light that was the next thing they saw. It would be his light that let them know they would make it through this.

Another huge boom echoed throughout the night and the sky lit up with not one, but two strikes of lightning in close proximity. When it struck and illuminated the property, Cate and her family watched in horror as they saw not one, but two silhouettes standing outside the barn.

11

"**D**ad!" Cate yelled, her voice full of fright now. "Someone's there!"

Ron had been facing his family. He hadn't seen the figure behind him. Joey had seen it and he began to bark ferociously, tearing out into the night after the uninvited guest.

"What?" Ron asked, confused.

"Someone else is there! We saw someone standing right behind you!" Cate yelled. "It looked like a man. Watch out!"

Cate was at a total loss as to what to do. Her mind raced as she thought about how this person must be the same one who was standing in the tree line at Mick's funeral. He must have been following her. She *knew* someone had been following her. But she had no idea what to do right now. If someone was trying to hurt them, then every decision Cate and her family made in the next few moments would be critical to their very survival.

"My God, Ron," Ellen called out. "Be careful!"

Cate frantically pulled her mobile phone out of her pocket. As she suspected, there was no service. Most likely because of the storm.

Lightning flashed again and Ron noticed something that was just out of sight for the rest of them. Cate, Ellen, and the kids could see the look of protectiveness flash across Ron's face. His brows were lowered and his eyes narrowed. He stood up straighter and looked fit and strong. He looked like he could handle anyone who dared to threaten his family. Her father's determination made Cate feel better, but she was scared for all of them. She wanted desperately to call Neil and to have him show up with some other officers and find out who was here watching them in the night and the storm. It *had* to be the same person who had been following her. There was no other logical explanation.

"I see him! He's running away. I'm going after him," Ron called out as he dashed into the storm. He didn't hesitate. Cate heard her father's umbrella whizzing around in the air as he went. It was the only object Ron had in his hands and he intended to use it as a weapon. Cate wondered why he hadn't taken time to step back inside and pick up some tools, but she dared not question his decision. She was glad he was here to protect them.

Ellen and Aaron made their way to where Cate was standing with the other two kids. It was slow going, but they felt their way across the barn until they made it. The five of them huddled together, afraid of what was happening outside.

Cate felt helpless. If she stayed in the barn with her kids, she was choosing to leave her dad alone to face the person who had been following her. She thought it wasn't fair that her dad be put in danger when the person following her most likely wasn't interested in him. He was caught in the crosshairs. If Cate left the barn to help her dad, she'd be leaving her kids alone and risking them losing the only parent they had left. The choice was obvious. It was no choice at all, really. Cate had to stay with the kids and keep them safe. She hated feeling helpless like this. She hated feeling like she was a victim, knocked down and just waiting to be victimized again and again. She wanted to do something, but her hands were tied. She was backed into a corner. It was a terrible feeling.

"The rifle is up at the house," Ellen whispered to Cate. "We keep it in case predators come around and try to harm our animals. We don't even keep the clip in the same place as the gun for safety reasons. But both pieces are up there. I know exactly where they are. I think I should go get them."

"Grandma, no!" Jilly said. "No guns."

Cate knew it was time to be decisive. Her mom was thinking clearly and using good judgment. Cate knew she had to do so as well.

"Jilly," Cate said to her daughter. "This is the time to take action. Your grandpa is out there running after someone who is sneaking around on the farm. No one should be out here at all. We don't know if that person is trying to hurt us or not. We need to do everything we can to protect ourselves."

"I agree, Mom," Aaron said. "Do it."

Cate could hardly bear the thought of leaving her

kids, but she also didn't want to send her mother out to retrieve the weapon. Cate was younger and in better physical condition. As a result, she was more likely to get the gun and return unharmed. She decided to go up to the house herself.

"I'll go," Cate said.

"Oh, honey," Ellen said to her daughter. "Let me go."

Cate's kids were silent. They could tell by the tone in her voice that she was serious and that her mind was made up. The kids also wanted Cate to go because they wanted her to protect them. They might not have been able to consciously understand the feelings and what each one meant, but something in each of the three of them responded to the strength their mom was exhibiting.

"I'll be better able to get back unharmed," Cate said to her mom. "It's decided. I'm going. Tell me where the rifle and the clip are."

Ellen told her daughter where to find the weapon, as requested. With the location of the rifle and the clip known, Cate hugged her children briefly and pushed them towards their grandmother. Then she walked calmly over to her father's toolbox and picked up a wrench and a crowbar to carry with her. She turned, and without hesitation, walked out of the barn and into the dark, raging storm, determined to do whatever was necessary to face her fears and her stalker head-on.

She moved quickly as she scrambled up the path and up the hill to the house. Her legs wobbled, but she carried on as if they didn't. She tried not to think too long or too hard about what might be happening with her dad right now. Instead, she became hyper-focused on getting into the house and finding the weapon. The power to the house had been knocked out, too. Everything was dark.

As she opened the back door, she wished Joey was here with her to sniff out and bark at any intruders who might be inside. Although she was glad that Joey had torn off after the intruder with her dad. She really wished Mick was there with her to take care of all of this. He was tall and strong and had looked like a formidable threat. She was certain that whoever was on the property and following her would back off if Mick was around to intervene. Cate took a deep breath, wiped a tear that had trickled down her cheek, and moved on.

Quickly, Cate felt her way through the dark house and located what she had come for. She placed the clip into the rifle then cocked it, ready to fire. She burst out the back door into the heavy rain again and ran towards the barn. But she didn't stop when she reached the others, except to ask if they were still okay. When they said they were, she took off in the direction her dad had gone, ready to do her part.

Joey barked in the distance and Cate assumed he was barking at the intruder. She followed the sound down the gravel road that ran alongside the Tatum's vineyard. Gravel gave her better footing on which to run, so she did so faster and harder. She panted as she ran, her lungs suffering under the level of exertion she was subjecting them to.

"Dad!" Cate called out as she neared the sound of Joey's barking. Lightning continued to strike and thunder barreled in the sky. Mother Nature showed no sign of letting up on the onslaught. "Dad!" she tried again. "I have the rifle."

Just as Cate got close enough to see her father's silhouette standing in front of her lightning lit up the sky and she spotted a pair of red tail lights glimmering in the distance.

"I couldn't keep up with him," Ron said, leaning over with his hands on his knees and trying to catch his breath. "I tried, but he had too much of a head start on me. He got away."

Cate leaned the rifle on the ground with one hand and used her other arm to wrap around her father's shoulders. Joey sat obediently by Ron's side, weathering the storm with his master.

"Don't feel bad," Cate told her dad. "It was very brave of you to run out after the guy. I'm just glad you're not hurt."

"Yeah," Ron said, disappointed that he wasn't able to catch him. "And look at my Cate Bear, out here in the rain with a rifle. That was very brave of you."

Cate leaned over and used both arms to hug her dad, letting the rifle drop all the way to the ground with a thud. Ron straightened up and wrapped his arms around his daughter. The two of them remained in an embrace for a long while as the rain fell, the thunder crackled, and the lightning periodically illuminated the sky. It had been years since Cate had hugged her father so tightly. It reminded her of being a little girl when she had been small enough to be carried. She remembered being held by her father as she leaned her head on his strong shoulders without a care in the world. She had been a

Daddy's girl. The two of them had been very close. They were still close, but the physical distance between them during the years the Brady family lived away had caused more of an emotional distance than Cate would have liked. She cried softly as her dad held her.

"What can I do, Cate Bear?" Ron asked.

"I think I'm in danger," Cate said as she raised her head to look at her dad's face. "Me and the kids."

"Because of this?" Ron asked. "For all we know, this was random. This guy didn't seem to be aggressive. Maybe he was lost. Maybe he was not in his right mind because alcohol or drugs. Who knows?"

"It's more than just this," Cate said. Then she told her dad about the figure at the cemetery, the knocked over trash cans the night of the funeral, and the dark-colored sedan which had been following her earlier that day. She told him everything, standing right there in the rain. She told him about Nancy and her claim that Mick had borrowed a lot of money. She told him about her mother-in-law's threat to call in the loan, which would mean that Cate and the kids would lose the house. She told him about Neil and his tense conversation with James right before he questioned her and told her that Mick's death might not have been an accident. It felt good to get it all out and to see the concern in her dad's eyes. Cate thought maybe the rain could somehow wash it all away. Maybe standing outside in the storm and telling her dad everything would convince fate to go easy on her. She was doing her best. She didn't know if she had it in her to do anything more.

"Cate, I hope you know that you always have a place

right here with your mom and me," Ron said, wiping a strand of hair out of his daughter's eyes. "You and the kids can stay with us for as long as you like. We don't have a lot of money to offer you, but we have this land and this farm. What's ours is yours if you need it."

"Thank you, Dad," Cate said. "That's very kind of you to say. And I do know. I hope it doesn't come to that because I don't want to infringe on your quiet little farm here. But it means the world to know that you and Mom are here for us."

"You're going to get through this," Ron answered. "I know you will."

As quickly as it had begun hours earlier, the storm quieted down and started to dissipate. Realizing that the family members left in the barn were probably concerned about Cate and Ron's safety, the pair walked back to let everyone know they were okay.

Cate had gotten used to the darkness by this point and didn't mind it anymore. It was the least of her troubles. Her emotions had been all over the place in the span of a half-hour. She had experienced the highs of connecting with her parents during moments she'd never forget. And she had experienced the lows of fear and helplessness which had been piling up relentlessly in recent days.

Ron and Ellen still had goats to track down and power to restore. Plus, they all needed dinner. Cate surprised herself by focusing on those easier to solve problems despite the fact that a man had just been standing and watching them from a short distance away. But such had become her life. For tonight, she wanted nothing more than to get something to eat and then get home and into bed.

Ellen and Ron insisted they would handle things at the farm and that Cate shouldn't worry herself about it. They told her it wasn't the first time they'd had animals get out of their pens. And since Ron worked as a lineman, he had contacts at the power company who could lend him a generator if the power stayed out for long. Believing the Tatums could handle things on their own, Cate and the kids said goodbye to her parents, then ordered burgers through a drive-through at a fast-food restaurant. Luckily, the restaurant had power and the drive-through was open for business. Cate, Aaron, Jilly, and Niko scarfed their food down hungrily while sitting in their SUV in the parking lot. They were all shaken by what had happened in Ron and Ellen's barn, but their bodies insisted they must eat.

Cate kept a close watch for the dark-colored vehicle, which she knew would continue to follow her. There was no such vehicle in sight. But if someone was trying to hurt her, she would face them like she had tonight. Head on.

12

D etective Neil Fredericks was in the kitchen of his home on Sixth Street when the call came in. He had been digging through a junk drawer to find matches and candles. The power had gone out on his street and it looked like it would be some time before any lights came back on. As a bachelor who lived alone, Neil didn't need to fuss about it. But he figured he'd get some candlelight going and re-read one of his favorite sci-fi novels for a while before getting to bed.

He recognized the incoming number right away. It was the police station.

"Hello. Detective Fredericks here," he said, sounding official.

"Yes, sir," the voice on the other end of the line said. Neil recognized it as Devonte Rucker from dispatch. "It's Officer Rucker. I'm calling as a courtesy because I know you're working the Brady case."

"That's right. I am," Neil confirmed. "Has something happened?"

"It appears there has been a break-in at the Brady home on Flock Hollow Lane this evening. A neighbor called it in. Sean O'Brien. He said he knew something was wrong when he noticed the Brady family's Labrador roaming outdoors. He claimed the dog always stays indoors or in the fenced backyard. Mr. O'Brien said he went to the Brady home to investigate and found the front door wide open, but no one home. He backed away and called us without stepping inside. Responding officers are on their way to the scene now. That's all I know."

"Thank you, Rucker," Neil said. "I appreciate the heads up. Is the dog alright?"

"Yes," Devonte answered. "Mr. O'Brien called her into his home and she's secure."

Neil thanked officer Rucker again and hung up the phone. Then he got into his car and headed for 19 Flock Hollow Lane.

13

As Cate drove home, ready to change into dry clothes and settle under her warm bed covers for the evening, her mobile phone suddenly began to ding and buzz with alerts.

That's strange, she thought to herself.

Apparently, she had crossed back into an area where cellular service was up and running normally. She pulled over into an empty parking lot to look at the alerts more closely. The rain had died down to a drizzle.

Several of them were weather alerts and storm warnings which had now expired. One was a text from Sasha asking if she and the kids had made it through the storm alright. Three were missed calls from a local number Cate didn't recognize. And then, there were two voicemails from Sean O'Brien. Sensing that something was wrong, Cate put the phone up to her ear so her children couldn't hear the playback, then pushed play on voicemail number one.

"Cate, this is Sean," the first voicemail message began.

"I saw Meesha roaming around out in front of my house. She came to me when I called her and I have her inside my house now. I'm calling to see if you're up and would like me to bring her home. Call me back when you get this. Bye."

Cate was alarmed to hear that Meesha had gotten out and had been loose in the neighborhood, especially with the potential for downed power lines and other storm-related hazards. She thought Aaron and Jilly might have left her in the backyard by accident. There was no way Meesha could have gotten out of the house on her own.

"Aaron, Jilly, dears," Cate began, holding her mobile phone against her chest. "Do you remember if Meesha was inside when you left the house this evening and came out to the SUV? To ride to Grandma and Grandpa's with me and Niko."

"Yeah, Mom," Aaron replied with certainty. "She was inside and the doors were locked. You can ask Mr. O'Brien and Mitchell. They were there and saw us lock up when we all walked out together."

"Meesha was definitely inside, Mom," Jilly echoed.

"Interesting," Cate said, mostly to herself.

"Why?" Aaron asked. "Is something wrong with Meesha?"

"No, she's fine," Cate said. "Mr. O'Brien called and left me a message that said Meesha was loose in the neighborhood. He got her into his house safely, so she's not in harm's way. I just don't know how she would have gotten out."

The kids talked amongst themselves as Cate raised the

phone back to her ear and pushed play on the second voicemail message from Sean O'Brien.

"Cate, it's Sean again. Listen, I went to your house when I didn't get you by phone last time, thinking I'd deliver Meesha back to you. But when I got there, things weren't right. I saw that you weren't home yet. Don't be alarmed, but I've called the police to check things out. Your front door was wide open. I think someone had been in the house. Police are on their way. Call me when you get this."

Cate's entire body flushed hot with rage as she listened to Sean's message. She was angry and wondered how someone dare go into her home. This escalated things to an entirely new level. Her pulse quickened as she thought about what to do next. She couldn't take the kids home when she didn't even know what she would find when she got there. She needed to know they would be safe somewhere. She needed to get them settled for the night, and fast so she could get home and handle things.

She considered taking the kids to Sasha's since she knew the power was still out at Ron and Ellen's, but she decided they wouldn't be very comfortable there. Sasha was Cate's friend. The kids didn't know her all that well. Next, she thought about taking the kids to her brother's house. They'd be comfortable with him and Rebecca, that's for sure, but she hadn't told James any of what had been going on lately and she didn't have time to fill him in now. She thought again about taking them back to her parents' house as she weighed her options. Whether or not the power had come back on, Ron and Ellen had already proven this evening that they would protect the kids at any cost. But the power was most certainly still out and Cate doubted her parents would have been able to get the goats back in yet. Besides, the damage to their barn would be a lot to deal with, and for all they knew, they were missing more than just Fred and Ginger. Cate figured it would be a night with very little sleep and she knew she probably shouldn't lean on her parents any more. She would have to ask James and Rebecca. It was the only reasonable option.

Cate texted her brother rather than call him, so her kids wouldn't know the details of what was going on. She didn't want them to be afraid. She told James there had been a possible break-in at her house while she and the kids were away for the evening and that she needed to get them situated somewhere for the night while she handled it. He replied immediately to bring them on over. He didn't ask any questions, for which she was grateful. Cate told the kids simply that she would take them to their Uncle James and Aunt Rebecca's house to spend the night because there was something she had to take care of at home. They asked a few questions, but she convinced them to wait for more details, saying she'd let them know as soon as she got there and checked it out. She drove the short distance to her brother's house and took her kids inside. Rebecca was warm and inviting and promised the kids they could make some popcorn and watch a movie together in the den. Cate hurried away, kissing the cheeks of each of her children and hoping that the next conversation she had with them would not disrupt their delicate lives any further.

As she pulled up to her house on Flock Hollow Lane,

Cate wasn't prepared for how much the sight of police cars and their blue flashing lights would unnerve her. She had experienced too much trauma in a short time and the damned blue light made it all feel worse. Cate's fear took over. She imagined several scenarios in which the blue lights had arrived to devastate her life.

First, Cate imagined that a police car had arrived to inform her of another loved one's death. It didn't make any logical sense, because she knew her remaining loved ones were all safe and accounted for tonight. But the fear of another horrible loss lingered.

Next, Cate imagined police officers had come to arrest her for her husband's murder and to take her away from her kids when they needed her most. She wasn't sure how likely that scenario was. And she knew that if she were to be arrested, she would be entitled to a trial. Though she worried about having enough money to pay for a good attorney, she hoped she'd have a decent chance in front of a jury of her peers. But regardless of how likely or unlikely either of those scenarios was, Cate's fears were very real. She had reason to think they were a possibility.

Finally, her mind landed on the more likely scenario for tonight's situation, that the person who had been following her had come to her home to harm her and the kids. When she heard Ron say that the man he chased didn't seem aggressive, it had given her a measure of comfort. But not comfort enough. Cate was becoming more and more certain that her husband's death had not been an accident and that whoever was responsible was now after her. She wondered if that person would try to kill her like they had Mick. She wondered if they would try to harm her children.

Cate took a few deep breaths as she pulled into the driveway, mentally preparing herself for whatever was to come. The lights were on at her house indicating the power lines were intact, so that was good.

Police tape covered Cate's front walkway. Officers were going in and out of her home through both the front and the garage doors. As she climbed the steps to her front porch, she couldn't help but think how what was once a happy part of her home used to greet loved ones had now turned into a harbinger of bad news and dread. However, she was happy to see a familiar face standing on the porch. It was Neil. He had heard her pull in the driveway and was coming out to meet her hoping he could help make this a little less overwhelming.

"Cate," Neil said kindly. "I'm sorry that you have to find out about all of this, well, like this. Where are the kids?"

"One of my neighbors called me. When I got his voicemail, I took the kids to my brother's. What's going on?"

"Your house has been broken into and robbed," Neil explained. "I'm just glad you weren't here when it happened. I shudder to think…"

"You and me both," Cate replied before he could finish his thought. "Can I go in?"

"Yes, certainly," Neil said, motioning for Cate to join him on the porch and then showing her through the front door. "It looks bad. I know it's hard to see your home like this."

He wasn't kidding. Things were a mess. Glass decor items were shattered all over the floor. Picture frames were knocked off the wall and tossed around. The flat-screen television was busted. And it looked like someone had been searching through drawers.

"You said robbed, right?" Cate managed to ask. "If we were robbed, why did they destroy the TV instead of taking it?" Cate was proud of herself for keeping enough of a level head to have asked.

"Good question," Neil said, agreeing with Cate. "Perhaps I should rephrase that. I suppose we should just say that your house was broken into, rather than saying it was robbed. We won't know for sure until you provide us a complete inventory of everything that was inside."

Teams of people in police department uniforms walked in and out of Cate's house, some carrying bags of evidence with them. Others took photos with loud flashes. Cate felt violated at having them rifling through her family's personal things. She didn't like strangers being in their personal space. As if they hadn't already been through enough.

"Who are all these people?" she asked Neil. "Why are they in my house?"

"Some of them are part of our forensics team," Neil explained. "They're dusting the house for prints and collecting other evidence which will hopefully provide DNA from the intruder. Others are detectives, like me, who are recording details of the crime scene to make sense of what happened here."

"Isn't this all a bit much for a break-in?" Cate asked.

Neil took Cate by the arm and guided her to a quiet

part of the living room where they wouldn't be overheard. He leaned down and spoke softly, his piercing blue eyes threatening to make Cate go weak in the knees. Cate hated being so susceptible to Neil's charms, but having him talk to her like this, over to the side, made her feel special.

"We're working a larger case here," he said. "We don't think this was just a break-in. There's almost certainly more to it. We don't know how the pieces add up yet, but we will figure them out in due time."

Cate did her best to remain calm and collected, both for her own sake and because she didn't want Neil to think she was weak. She leaned back against the wall near where they were standing and closed her eyes as she tried to think. It was nearly ten o'clock by now and she'd had a very long day. She wondered who could have done this. And why? The only thing that made any sense to her now was the realization that she and her kids truly were in danger. She hated to think what might have happened if they had been home. Her mind reeled as she tried to figure out where they could take refuge. Her parents' house had seemed like a safe place, but after seeing the man her father had to chase off in the rainstorm tonight, she wasn't so sure anymore.

"Cate," Neil said quietly. He sounded like he didn't want anyone else to hear what he was about to say. "We will have to ask you more questions. I want you to be prepared for what's coming."

"More questions?" Cate asked. Her voice shook as the words came out. She could tell that the police suspected her involvement. Sickness twisted her insides. She began to think she really needed to get a lawyer.

"Yes, I'm afraid so," Neil replied. "There's no avoiding it."

"Can that wait until the morning, at least?" Cate asked. It had been an incredibly long day and she didn't know how much more she could take. She *needed* until the morning to get herself together. She needed to determine how she would respond. She needed to phone a lawyer.

"Probably, yes," Neil said. "I'll see what I can do to delay things. But I want you to be prepared. They're building a case and, I know this is hard to hear, but they have evidence that points to you having had some involvement in your husband's death."

"They?" Cate asked, anger simmering under her skin. "Aren't you part of that group?"

Neil looked hurt, but Cate continued, her voice getting louder. She didn't care if her anger made Neil upset. She wasn't so sure he was on her side, anyway.

"You are an investigator with the Rosemary Run Police Department, correct?"

"It isn't like that," Neil said, raising a finger to encourage Cate to lower her voice. He stepped closer to her and she got a whiff of his aftershave again. His alluring, masculine smell made it hard for her to stay mad at him.

"Look," Neil said. Cate could tell he was trying to be kind. At least, she thought so. "We're almost done here. I'll hang around afterward and we will talk more then. Sound okay?"

Cate liked the idea of being able to talk to Neil alone.

She wanted to tell him about the man that her dad had chased off earlier in the evening. "Yes," she said. "I have something I want to say."

It took nearly two more hours before police investigators were finished sorting through and collecting evidence from the Brady family home. It was almost midnight and Cate was more exhausted than she thought she had ever been in her life. She wasn't sure she would make it in to work on time tomorrow, so she emailed her boss, Laura, to let her know that she expected to need ongoing flexibility with her day-to-day schedule. Cate also messaged the kids' school, because she knew they weren't likely to make it there at all tomorrow. They didn't have clean clothes over at James and Rebecca's. Cate would need to take them a bag or else bring them home to clean up and get dressed. After the evening they'd all had, she decided it would be best for them to sleep in and take it easy. Rebecca was an accountant who worked primarily from home on her own time. She could probably adjust her schedule to hang out with the kids in the morning. Cate hated to ask Rebecca to extend herself in that way, but she needed the help.

Once again, their lives had come to a grinding halt. They would need to stop and collect themselves as they tried to figure out the next steps. Cate resented the way her family was being tossed about from one dramatic scene to another. Their formerly peaceful lives had turned into anything but. Cate hardly knew which threat to address first. She felt like she was working blind, stumbling through a fog that was so thick and so enveloping she couldn't see her way out.

Neil kept his promise and stayed after the others had left. He saw his colleagues out and told them he'd file his report in the morning after he wrapped some things up. As he closed the door and turned around to face Cate, she began to feel conflicted. She wanted him to stay. She wanted to be near him. But she didn't want to do anything that would seem inappropriate or that might implicate her further. It was best to keep things business-like with the police department. Although, when Neil Fredericks looked at her with those blue eyes, Cate feared it was already too late for that.

"There," Neil said. "Now it's just you and me. Let's sit down and you can tell me whatever it is you wanted to say."

Cate nodded, then motioned to the sofa in the living room. Some police department employees had been sitting on it, so it was clear of debris. Cate sat on one end and Neil sat down on the other. Cate felt a little odd to be sitting with a handsome, single man on the living room sofa that she and Mick had picked out together. It had been in the family for years.

"What do you make of this?" Cate asked. She didn't want to start with the story about the man at her parents' farm. She preferred to try and find out what Neil knew first. It seemed to Cate like Neil found her attractive and it occurred to her that perhaps she could use Neil's interest to her advantage. She aimed to find out everything he knew.

"It's hard to say until forensic results come back," Neil replied. "I think there's much more to the story. And I don't think it's over yet."

"Forgive me," Cate began, getting right to the point. "But I need to figure out how to keep my kids safe. I don't have time for formalities and niceties. I need to know exactly what's going on so I can figure out what to do. Their lives are on the line here. Those three souls depend on me to look out for them. They're not old enough to make decisions for themselves. I owe it to them to do my very best. Will you help me by telling me what you know, please?"

Cate reached up and slowly took her long, blonde hair down from the tie that had been holding it back. Cate was a beautiful woman, and she knew it. Although she had been married for most of her adult life, she knew the way men noticed her. How they watched her when they didn't think she was looking, and how they responded to her movements. Mick had known it, too. He'd never seemed to mind. Cate liked to think Mick would approve of her using her feminine charms if it meant gaining an advantage to keep her and the kids safe.

Neil looked down at the floor, absentmindedly smoothing the middle sofa cushion between them. He wanted to help Cate. He was thinking about how to do it. It was the first time Neil Fredericks had found himself conflicted about his duty as a police officer and his obligation to the oath he took. He had told his partner that he would gain Cate's trust to get her to cooperate with their investigation, but he was beginning to have feelings for her and he didn't want to put her in harm's way. He felt confused by the feelings he was experiencing. After all, it had been only a single day that he'd spent time with Cate and had gotten to know her as more than an acquaintance. It felt like it had been much longer. Neil felt like he had known Cate Brady forever.

Neil knew things he could tell her, if he were going to pledge his loyalty to her, that is. He began to imagine his life as something other than a police officer. He never wanted to leave the force. He had always thought of himself retiring as an investigator when he was an old man. But if it meant that he had to leave the force to gain a love who would make his life complete, he figured he would happily switch to a new profession. He thought maybe he could open his own private investigation business. Neil began to imagine what it would be like to date someone who had three grieving children to tend to and what it might be like to hold Cate Brady in his arms.

"Hey, what was your maiden name?" Neil asked. "Who were you before Brady?"

"I was Cate Tatum," she said without hesitation. "But surely you know that. You know my brother."

"Yeah, right," Neil said, looking embarrassed now. He was becoming frazzled. He had surprised himself with his mistake. He felt like a giddy schoolboy, taken with a beautiful girl.

Cate began to blush, too. The attraction between the two of them was becoming undeniable. It was magnetic. "What made you think about my maiden name?" she asked. "Are you planning to run some super-secret background check on me?" She was kidding, but she also hoped he wasn't actually going to do that.

"You tell me, Cate Tatum," Neil joked. "Should I run a super-secret background check on you?"

Cate liked the way he was using her maiden name.

Neil suddenly became more serious. "I'm sorry," he said. "I don't mean any disrespect to your husband or your marriage. I shouldn't be using your maiden name that way."

"It's okay," Cate said. And it really was. She appreciated Neil's awareness of her feelings, but it was a thrill to be called Cate Tatum again. It made her feel young. Like life was full of possibilities.

Neil shifted on the sofa so that one arm leaned along the back and his body turned towards Cate. In his new position, he was much closer to her.

"What did you want to tell me, anyway?" Neil asked.

Cate had wanted to learn what Neil knew first, but he was holding back. She decided she had better go ahead and tell him about the man at her parents' house.

"Yeah, that," she said, crossing one leg over the other so her body stretched further in Neil's direction. "Something happened while I was at my parents' farm tonight."

"Dare I ask what?"

"A strange man was there. My dad chased the guy away, but wasn't fast enough to catch him."

Neil lowered his eyebrows. He was obviously concerned and upset. Cate liked to see him with this expression of concern. "Did you get a look at the guy?"

"No," Cate said. "All I can tell you is that he was about the height of my dad. The power was out, and it was pitch black. Rain was pouring down and visibility was low. We were in the barn tending to the animals when lightning struck a tree outside and it came crashing down onto one wall. The goats got out of their pen and it was a big mess.

My kids were scared of the dark and the storm. Thunder and lightning were all around us."

"I'd ask about your parents having goats because that sounds adorable, but I'm more concerned about how the strange man came into play," Neil said, leaning forward towards Cate.

"The goats are adorable," Cate said with a smile. "My parents also have sheep, cows, chickens, and a cool black and white dog named Joey. Their place is a regular little farm. It's out on Pleasant Valley Road."

Neil smiled in response to Cate's smile. He liked seeing her face lit up. He imagined that it must light up a lot more when things aren't so tumultuous in her life. He thought he'd like to be around to see that.

"Nice," he said. "But the guy?" Neil reached forward with his hand, which had been resting on the back of the couch, out towards Cate and placed it gently on her shoulder. She turned and looked up at him with her big brown eyes. Neil let his hand linger there for a moment. He could feel his body responding to the electricity sparking between them.

Cate broke the gaze first, looking down at the floor while she spoke. "My dad was in the doorway to the barn, preparing to go up to the house and look for a flashlight or lantern. We were all turned towards the sound of his voice because we knew that's the direction we should watch for the light. We knew he'd be bringing it back with him when he returned. Lightning struck twice and lit up the sky so brightly that we could see everything for a moment. There in the doorway was a man standing a short distance behind my dad."

"He was just standing there?" Neil asked, surprised.

"Yes, it was terribly frightening. I yelled at my dad to tell him someone was there. My dad didn't hesitate. As soon as he understood what I was saying, he took off after the guy. Joey, the dog, went too."

"But they didn't get him?"

"No," Cate confirmed. "The guy got a head start once he realized I'd seen him. I guess with all the rain and thunder and lightning and mud, Dad and Joey just couldn't get to him fast enough. I had gone into the house to get my parents' rifle. By the time I got back with it and caught up to my dad, we saw red taillights in the distance driving off of their property."

"Let me guess," Neil said. "A dark-colored, full-size sedan?"

"As far as I could tell, yes," Cate said. "It was too dark to confirm the color, but it was definitely a car."

Neil sighed heavily and appeared saddened by this news. He looked like he was worried about Cate's safety.

"Are you planning to stay here alone tonight?" Neil asked, scooting forward and placing his hand on Cate's back, between her shoulder blades.

Cate trembled at his touch. She tilted her head to one side, trying to keep her composure.

"I think so, yes," she said. "If the guy following me was in all the places I think he was, then he could probably find me no matter where I go. He seemed to already know my patterns and movements. Besides, I have a gun here. The kids don't know about it, but I keep a handgun locked in the top of the closet. I could get it out and sleep with it on my nightstand, just for tonight." Cate had almost said that she and Mick kept a gun in the closet. She thought it a small victory to have left his name out and spoken only for herself.

"I'm worried about you," Neil said, finally articulating the words Cate had hoped to hear. "I don't like you being alone tonight."

Cate leaned forward towards Neil, looking him right in his gorgeous blue eyes. She felt like she was in a strange dream. Or like she was having a dramatic out-of-body experience. None of this felt real. It hadn't since Mick died. She had been thrust into an unpredictable landscape that she wasn't equipped to navigate. She felt like a young, single woman again. The kind of woman who had only begun to get going at midnight each night. The kind of woman willing to take risks. The kind of woman who would kiss Neil Fredricks.

Cate opened her mouth to speak, but only a soft moan came out. The attraction she felt to Neil was irresistible. Giving in to passion, Cate leaped into Neil's lap, her legs straddling his waist and her arms wrapping tightly around his neck. He didn't push her away. Instead, he wrapped his large, muscular arms around her body and pulled her to him. The pair stopped short just as their lips were about to meet and looked intently into each other's eyes for a moment more, as if to solidify their decision. When Cate felt Neil's lips against her own, her body relaxed for the first time in a very long time. She became putty in his hands, every touch taking her to depths she hadn't even imagined. They took their clothes off piece by piece and made tender, passionate love on Cate's living room sofa until they fell asleep, exhausted and happy.

14

"My God, Cate," James said. He had let himself in with his key.

Neil and Cate had been sleeping, naked, on the sofa. They were still out cold when James walked in, despite morning sun shining brightly through the windows.

"James!" Cate said as her weary eyes focused on her brother.

"Look at you," he said to his sister. "Wearing nothing but your wedding ring."

Cate was waking up quickly now, whether she liked it or not. She grabbed a sofa cushion and used it to cover herself as she reached for her clothes.

"Easy, James," Neil said. "This doesn't concern you."

"Doesn't concern me?" James said, the volume of his voice escalating. "I'd say it concerns me when you're taking advantage of my little sister. She's a grieving widow, for God's sake."

"James," Cate said. "I'm a grown woman and can

make my own decisions. I appreciate you looking out for me, but I can handle myself."

James turned around to give his sister privacy while she dressed. "I don't think you can handle yourself," he said. "Not if you're sleeping with Neil Fredericks. I don't think you have any idea what you've gotten yourself into."

"And just what is that supposed to mean?" Neil replied.

"You know what it means," James said, walking towards the detective as Neil worked to get dressed. James didn't seem to care that Neil was still half-naked. He was feeling protective of his little sister and was getting angry.

"Did he tell you?" James asked Cate.

"James, stop it," Neil said.

"I will not stop it. She's my sister and she deserves to know."

Cate stood up, fully dressed now. She was getting angry as well. "What are you talking about, James?" she asked.

"I still can't believe my eyes, Cate," James said, shaking his head from side to side. "What were you thinking? What if the kids had been with me?"

"I know how this looks," she replied. "But really, I think you're overreacting."

"Oh, really?" James asked, his tone becoming condescending. "What you don't know is that Neil and his buddy Luke are planning to arrest you for Mick's murder. When I talked to Neil yesterday morning at your office, they were one step away from bringing you in."

Cate's face felt hot and she tried to process this information.

"Is that true?" she asked Neil, turning towards him. He suddenly felt like a stranger again. Cate began to wonder if she had made a big mistake.

Neil looked at James and sighed heavily. "It's complicated." he said. "You know that, James. I'm not going to hurt your sister. My intentions here are good."

"The way I see it, you're in another man's house and you just slept with another man's wife. While she was wearing her wedding ring, no less. I'm not sure how you can feel good about your intentions unless there's something seriously wrong with you."

Cate was growing weary with her brother's grandstanding. She wanted Neil to answer the question.

"Neil, answer me, please," she pleaded. "Is what James is saying true? Are you and Luke planning to arrest me?"

Neil looked at Cate with a sad and conflicted expression. He didn't want to hurt her. It was true that his intentions were good. But it was also true that he and Luke were one step away from bringing her in, under arrest.

Cate raised her hand and covered her mouth in horror. The look on Neil's face gave her the answer she needed, whether she liked it or not. She paced around the house as she worked to absorb the shock, stepping over the mess as she went. James and Neil continued to argue in the background. Their voices seemed to drone on and were becoming a blur to Cate. She thought about how her current physical surroundings mirrored the state of her life. Both were in shambles.

Before she could collect herself enough to say anything else, there was a knock at the door. Cate, Neil, and James all looked at each other. Neil was still shirtless and knew this looked bad. James also knew it looked bad, yet seemed eager for the chance to rub it in and embarrass his colleague. James went straight to the front door and opened it.

It was Sean O'Brien, bringing Meesha back home. Cate quickly tousled her hair with her fingers and straightened her clothing to try and look as presentable as possible, then she walked to the front door to thank her neighbor. She stepped in front of her brother, taking over and trying to act normal. Neil's car was still in the driveway.

"Sean!" Cate said. "Thank you so much for taking care of our girl and for bringing her home."

"It's no problem at all," Sean said, unhooking Meesha's collar from a makeshift lead he had fashioned out of rope. "I'm happy to help." Cate knew Sean could tell that things seemed off as he leaned his neck to one side to get a glimpse of what was happening. "Are the kids home this morning?"

Cate didn't know what time it was. She wasn't sure if Mitchell would have left for school already or not. It felt early, but maybe that was just because she had been awake so late the night before.

"They're at my house this morning with Rebecca," James offered. "After what happened last night, we thought they'd be safer over there."

"Yeah, that makes sense," Sean said. "I told Mitchell not to expect Jilly or Aaron on the bus today. I knew you had a late night." Sean leaned further in the door and gave a knowing look to Neil as if he understood exactly what was going on. Cate felt herself blush.

"Well, thanks again," Cate said, beginning to close the front door.

"Wait!" Sean implored as he placed one hand up to stop the door from closing all the way.

"Yes?" Cate said, her brother standing by her side. They both waited to hear what Sean had to say.

"Last night," Sean said. "The police were asking me a lot of strange questions that I thought you should know about."

Cate became uncomfortable with how things were unfolding. Everything seemed to assault her senses. The sun was bright as it shone in from the open door and windows. The air was cold. It felt like last night's storms had brought in cooler temperatures again. Cate wanted things to be gentle. She wanted things to move slowly. She wanted to have more time to absorb what was happening and to decide how she would cope.

"Oh?" she asked, not really wanting to hear what he had to say right now.

"Yeah," Sean said. He seemed strangely excited by whatever it was he was about to tell them. It reminded Cate of the day of Mick's funeral when Sean had seemed too upbeat for the occasion. It suddenly struck Cate that something was strange about Sean O'Brien. He had been the one who had found the house open. She wondered if he might have had something to do with the break-in.

"Sean, I appreciate you looking out for me, but if you don't mind, I'd like to talk about this a little later," Cate said. Meesha sat dutifully at her side as Cate stroked the top of the dog's head. Cate thought about how Meesha was helping to center her. She knew Meesha must have smelled the scent of all the different people who had been in their home. She must have also seen how many things were out of place and broken. Yet, the dog had chosen to stick with Cate rather than walk around the house to check it out. Cate was grateful for Meesha's friendly and loyal presence.

"I don't think this should wait," Sean said.

Cate looked at her brother, who shrugged his shoulders. She didn't look at Neil. She didn't want to draw attention to his presence, especially because he was still shirtless. But she was nervous that what Sean might say could get her into more trouble with the police. She didn't know why exactly, but she felt like there might be a conflict. Cate had been close to telling Sean to go ahead with whatever he wanted to relay to her until something inside told her to stick to her guns and to make him wait. She gathered her energy and drew a firm line.

"Thanks again, Sean, but this needs to wait until later. I'll be in touch by the end of the day. Promise." Cate closed the door, despite Sean's protests. He looked offended, but Cate didn't care. He was the least of her problems.

Cate knew she needed to tell her brother everything that had happened. She'd been meaning to fill him in for days now, but things had been piling up. She knew she needed her brother's guidance. She needed to know how he'd heard about her pending arrest and why he hadn't told her sooner. She needed to figure out who she could trust.

After Sean left the porch and walked down the sidewalk towards his own home, Neil bowed out of the situation and let Cate and her brother be. He excused himself, promising to get in touch with Cate soon. He walked out to his car and drove away.

Cate felt conflicted as she watched him go. She had enjoyed their time together last night and had found herself considering what a relationship with him might be like. The rational part of her knew she needed to temper that enthusiasm. The rational part of her knew she needed to prepare for her own arrest.

15

"I need a good lawyer, and quick," Cate said to her brother once Neil's car had left the driveway and the two of them were alone.

"I hate to say it," James affirmed. "But I think you might be right. This whole thing is a disaster."

Cate nodded and gestured with one hand to their surroundings.

"I had nothing to do with his death, you know," Cate said. She didn't think she had to say it, but she figured she might as well to clear the air.

"I know that," James confirmed. "I'm not the one you should proclaim your innocence to."

"I get it," Cate replied. She didn't need James to spell it out for her, but he did anyway.

"That might be a good statement to make to your new friend, Detective Fredericks."

"Can we just skip that whole topic right now?" Cate implored. "Please?"

"I don't know, sis. I have some serious concerns about

your judgment. I feel like I have a responsibility to look after you."

"Yeah? Well, how about you look into what the police have on me? Because I can't imagine what it is. And while you're at it, look into the person who is following me and who broke into my home. If you really want to look after me, that's what you can do." Cate was getting irritated now. She didn't like the way her brother was acting self-righteous when he didn't even know the whole story.

"I can't just go in and find out everything about the investigation surrounding you," James said. "They're keeping me at a distance from that because you're my sister. At this point, they need to be keeping Neil Fredericks at a distance from it as well. I'm not sure how you think either of us can tell you what you want to know. The police department has strict procedures and guidelines. They don't just go around sharing information willy-nilly."

"Willy-nilly?" Cate asked. They both laughed. It was good to break the tension.

James put his hands on his hips. The way he was standing with the morning light shining on his face from the side, Cate thought he looked a lot like their dad. Her mind wandered, and she imagined how nice it would be for James to continue to look after her, even after their dad grew old and died. She appreciated her brother feeling protective of her the same way she appreciated her dad chasing down the guy in the barn last night. But she didn't want either of them trying to run her life, either.

"What is your problem with Neil, anyway?" Cate

asked, sitting down in an armchair. It felt wrong to sit on the sofa, given what had just taken place there.

"I don't know," James replied. "I'm not saying he's a bad guy. I think mostly, I didn't expect you to jump into bed with somebody a week after your husband died. You were married for what, fifteen years? It's hard to remember you being with anybody but Mick."

Cate had hoped James would talk about Neil without bringing Mick into it. She didn't need or want moral judgment about her behavior. She decided to steer the conversation back to the investigation.

"Anyway," Cate said, rolling her eyes at her brother. "I'm serious that I want you to look into the investigation. Find out what they think I did. Even if they try to keep you at a distance, you find a way. I'm family."

"I know you're family," James said. "Surely you understand that I want to help. I just don't know if I can." His tone was kinder now, but they were still at odds with each other.

"Well, you can look into the guy who is following me. Right?" Cate said.

"What are you even talking about?" James asked. "What makes you think someone is following you?"

"I hadn't told you. But a lot has happened. Someone is definitely following me because he was at Mom and Dad's last night in the rainstorm. We all saw him."

James sat down in the armchair across from his sister and rested his elbows on his knees. He looked intense and concerned, but skeptical. "I'm listening," he said.

Cate repeated the story, the same way she had told Neil the night before. She also told her brother about feeling like she was being watched. She told him about the figure along the tree line at the cemetery, the knocked-over trash cans at the house the night of the funeral, and the dark-colored sedan behind her on her way home from work yesterday which then parked in the parking lot of Niko's preschool. She even told him about Pal, the homeless man, and how he seemed to know something about the way Mick died. When she was finished, James took a moment before he said anything.

"Okay," he said finally. "I'll look into it. But, Cate, I think the grief may be getting to you. As in, perhaps the stress is making you paranoid. We all know you've been under an inordinate amount of stress lately. I'm not trying to hurt your feelings, but I think you may be exaggerating these things in your mind."

"Are you serious right now?" Cate asked, getting angry again. "Don't talk down to me, James. I thought the same thing as you, at first, which is why I hadn't said anything until now. But so many things are stacking up. They can't all be a coincidence."

James considered her words, but still wasn't so sure.

Look," he said. "Let's start with a few surveillance cameras. If anyone comes around, then maybe we can catch them on camera."

"Neil mentioned that he has a friend who works at an alarm company," Cate said. "But I was hesitant to sign up for monitoring. I don't want to live in fear."

"I can understand that," James said. "But you and the kids need to be safe. What if, instead of a full alarm system which would be visible to intruders, we begin with hidden cameras? That way, if someone is after you, we have a better chance of finding out who they are."

"I like that idea," Cate said. "Fine then. I'll order a few security cameras online. I'll do it right now. Will you help me install them when they arrive?"

"Of course," James said. "Sign up for the fastest shipping you can. Let's get them turned on as soon as possible."

"Done," Cate said. In a matter of a few minutes, she had placed the order, then closed her laptop, feeling accomplished. "Now for an attorney. Do you know anyone?"

James shook his head. "No, thankfully, I haven't had occasion to hire an attorney. I think Rebecca may know one from school though. I'll ask her to send you a name."

"Excellent," Cate said. She felt strong having taken actions that could help resolve her issues. Nothing was worse than feeling completely helpless. "Now excuse me. I'm going to take a shower and head into work. I think it will do me good."

16

Cate phoned Rebecca on her way into work. She confirmed that her sister-in-law could, in fact, keep the kids for the day. Cate spoke briefly to Aaron, and he said they were all having a good time with board games and superhero movies. The kids were grateful to have the day out of school and agreed they needed some downtime to recharge. Cate dropped off a bag with clothes and toiletries so the kids could get cleaned up. She didn't ask Rebecca about an attorney. The kids were in close proximity and she didn't want to scare them. Cate knew that James had promised to ask, so she decided to give him some time to do it. Besides, she assumed that if she were to be arrested, she would post bail and could get in touch with a lawyer then.

Cate couldn't imagine what the police thought they had on her, anyway. She knew that maybe it was denial, but no matter how many times she told herself she should prepare to be arrested, she couldn't quite believe it. It sounded far-fetched and ridiculous.

Satisfied that Aaron, Jilly, and Niko were safe and happy, Cate turned her attention to other matters. She wanted to focus on things she felt like she could control. She wanted to focus on things she could make some progress on.

The day was bright and the stormy weather had subsided completely. Rays of light seemed to be shining almost sideways as the sun hung lower in the sky this time of year. Cate thought it was a perfect October day. It was cool, but not too cold. It was just the right temperature for Cate to wear a cozy sweater over top of her blouse and a pair of stylish tan boots up to her knees. There was a slight breeze, which was just enough to make the leaves rustle and crackle gently as they fell to the ground and swam around light posts and park benches. The nice weather made Cate feel hopeful. The changing seasons brought an energy which made her feel the pull of forward motion. There was an inevitability to it. Deep down, Cate knew that she couldn't resist moving forward any more than the leaves on the trees could resist their turn in the annual cycle of death and rebirth.

Her emotions seemed to vacillate from one extreme to the other. Feeling happy made her feel guilty. She didn't want to move on too quickly after Mick's death. She was concerned that doing so would mean dishonoring the love and the life that they had shared. On the other hand, Mick was a selfless guy who wanted the very best for his family. The two of them had never talked about it, but Cate knew he would want her to move on and be happy after his death.

Halloween was coming up in less than a week, and

Cate suddenly realized that she needed to help the kids get costumes together. She made a mental note to do just that. Aaron was too old for trick-or-treating now and Jilly was skirting the edge of that line, but Niko would want to go door-to-door while in costume. Perhaps the older kids would walk with him. Or maybe they'd stay at the house and give out candy. Either way, all three would want to dress up.

The kids hadn't mentioned Halloween since Mick died, but Cate knew they'd appreciate it if she made some plans. It wouldn't be right for them to skip the holiday. Mick wouldn't have wanted that. He had loved taking the kids trick-or-treating. He used to kick Halloween off each year by carving pumpkins into jack-o'-lanterns with the kids and then setting their creations out on the front porch with candles inside. Next, he'd help everyone into their costumes while playing spooky music in the background. Mick had always been good about making things fun. Cate remembered how he would place the little ones on his shoulders for a ride when they tired of walking. She had always thought there was nothing cuter than one of her toddlers on their daddy's shoulders while bundled up in a plush Halloween costume.

November would be here soon, too, and with it the start of the winter holidays. Cate had always loved this time of year. She and Mick usually cooked Thanksgiving dinner and hosted the rest of the extended family. They would typically start baking a full two days early. Cate would make her Grandma Tatum's from-scratch pie crust, which was always a hit. The night before Thanksgiving day, she and Mick would stay up late, drinking wine and preparing casseroles to be baked the next day. They'd fall into bed, exhausted, and make love by candlelight. It had become a tradition. When Turkey Day finally arrived, they'd wake up early with the kids, too excited to care that they had gotten little sleep. They'd all watch the Macy's Thanksgiving Day parade on TV together while they finished the final work on the holiday dinner. Extended family, and sometimes friends, would arrive in the late afternoon. They'd eat the bounty they had prepared so lovingly, then end the day positively glowing they were so happy.

The day after Thanksgiving always meant Christmas shopping in the Brady household. The five of them would get dressed up in festive attire and hit the mall for all the big sales. The things they bought weren't nearly as important as the time spent together. The fun always continued throughout December with hot chocolate, visits to see Santa, baking and decorating cookies, and festive gatherings. Cate thought it really was the most wonderful time of the year and she had successfully convinced her kids of the same. Christmas Eve always included more holiday meal prep, cookie decorating, matching family pajamas, stories told at bedtime, and the opening of one special gift. When Christmas morning finally arrived, they'd stumble downstairs, bleary-eyed and giddy with excitement to open presents. Most years, the Bradys hosted Christmas dinner for extended family, too. They enjoyed hosting and didn't mind the work it took. Family would come over for dinner, then they'd all sit around the fire and sing Christmas carols together. It was every bit as much fun as it sounded. Each member of the Brady family thoroughly enjoyed themselves every year.

Remembering their family traditions made Cate terribly sad at the thought of moving through the holidays without Mick. At the same time though, the season was associated with so many happy things that Cate thought she might just be able to get through it. She knew she needed to make the holidays positive for the kids. Sitting around feeling sorry for herself was not an option. It would be difficult, but she owed it to them to put in an effort. Maybe they could start new traditions together.

As she pulled into the parking garage near her office and parked her SUV, Cate took a few minutes to pretend that nothing was wrong in her life. Or, at least, like she had a fresh start and that things could be good again. Something about the storm and the nice weather that followed seemed to have cleansed her spirit. Or maybe it was something about her night with Neil. Either way, she was dreaming about being happy again.

Cate came up with little things she could do which would make things fun for her and the kids. For starters, she decided to get out their Halloween decorations from the attic and to spruce the house up. Especially after the break-in, Cate felt like it was important to reclaim the space as their own. What better way to do that than to decorate for the holiday? If the person who ransacked their home was watching, moving on to not only clean things up but to decorate the place seemed like a good message to send. It would be a show of strength.

Next, Cate turned her attention to the changing seasons and thought about what she would have been doing with the kids this last week of October if life had been normal. She knew she needed to go through Niko's winter clothes and figure out how much still fit from last year. At his age, he was growing so fast it was likely that very little was still wearable. Cate would need to do some shopping and make sure Niko had all the clothes he needed. She didn't think Jilly had grown very much in the past year, but her daughter would enjoy the chance to shop for some new clothes. Aaron would tag along reluctantly, whether or not he had outgrown last year's clothes. Cate knew shopping wouldn't be a teenage boy's favorite activity, but she also knew her son would like some new things, especially if they featured art from one of his favorite bands.

As Cate thought about other tasks she could tackle, work came to mind. The magazine typically ran about six months ahead from the time content needed to be created to when it would be published. That meant articles she worked on in the next few weeks would be slated to come out just as warmer temperatures and summer rolled around next year. Cate liked the idea of reaching that far into the future. She imagined what would be happening then. The kids would all be getting out of school for summer break. Niko would be finishing preschool and preparing to enter kindergarten in the fall. Jilly would have one more year in middle school and Aaron would be a rising sophomore in high school. Cate hated that Mick would miss seeing their kids grow and change. But she looked forward to being there to enjoy every minute herself.

Feeling positive, Cate began to think about ideas for

magazine articles. The town's newest winery, Valley Vineyards, had opened down by the bay. It was Cate's job to go and interview new businesses, particularly those which aimed to attract tourists. She'd take a photographer with her and visit the grounds, then write it up so the most positive parts of the story were highlighted. Much of her job was focused on making Rosemary Run look and sound attractive to those who might want to visit the quaint little town. Cate enjoyed her job, and she did it well. Vine Country Magazine was a wonderful place to work.

Bolstered by her visions for the future, Cate turned off the ignition in the SUV and stepped out into the October air. She knew there was a growing list of unpleasant things she should turn her attention to, such as digging into her finances and finding out whether Mick had life insurance. Or searching for a record of the debt Nancy claimed he owed and finding out if she was in jeopardy of losing her home. But Cate wasn't ready for those tasks yet. She needed to pretend for a while longer that everything would be okay.

She walked to the Brick House Cafe as usual and purchased two breakfast sandwiches and two cups of coffee. One for her and one for Pal. Hopefully he wasn't mad at her for getting forceful with him when they last spoke. She stepped out of the café and around the corner where she saw Pal sitting in his usual spot on a bench. Cate felt a little apprehensive when she laid eyes on him. She hoped that giving him today's coffee and a sandwich would help smooth things over. She still wanted to find out what he knew about Mick's death. She didn't even have to know right away. She had decided she could take things slow and wait for Pal to become comfortable enough to talk to her if that's what it took. After all, knowing wouldn't bring her husband back from the dead.

"Pal! Good morning," Cate said, picking up her pace as she approached the homeless man.

"Hi, there," he replied. He reached out his hand and gratefully received the coffee and sandwich. As usual, he opened the sandwich quickly and scarfed the food down. He was hungry. "Thank you," he managed in between bites. He didn't seem upset over what had happened between them. Cate suspected that he might have had some kind of mental break when he had begun muttering. And if so, maybe he wouldn't even remember what had happened. Cate knew she was no expert, but hoped she could keep the man calm.

"You're very welcome," Cate said. She sat down beside Pal on the bench and waited while he ate.

"I saw your husband," Pal said nonchalantly as he chewed.

"Yeah, I remember," Cate said as she looked straight ahead, people watching. "I think you met him more than once, actually. He used to come here and meet me for lunch sometimes."

"At Lorraine's Diner," Pal added.

"What?" Cate asked. "I don't think Mick ever saw you at Lorraine's. At least, he didn't mention it to me." Pal seemed lucid, but Cate thought what he was saying wasn't making much sense. She thought he must have been confused.

"Yes, ma'am," Pal continued. "Lorraine's Diner, yesterday. He was talking with Tim, Lorraine's son, who owns the place." Cate felt a chill run up and down her spine when she heard Pal say those words. She thought that if he were trying to toy with her or to play a joke, it wasn't funny. Without consciously realizing it, Cate turned her body away, shifting her weight in the other direction.

"Pal," she said, not looking at him. "You know my husband passed away. I'd appreciate it if you didn't say things like that. I find it disrespectful. I *really* don't like it."

"Yes, ma'am," he said, balling up his empty sandwich wrapper and moving on to the hot coffee.

The two of them sat silently as Cate considered whether to try and question him. She figured Pal's comment about seeing Mick at Lorraine's only proved his level of delusion. And that meant that his comments from the previous day about knowing how Mick died were probably off base. Maybe Pal had lost touch with reality. Cate knew it was a sad fact that homeless people were often mentally ill. She didn't want to get into another hostile exchange with Pal, but a part of her thought maybe what he had said could be true. Could Mick be alive? Cate felt dizzy as she tried to make a case in her mind for the possibility. She wondered if the man at her parents' farm last night might have had something to do with this. She remembered what her dad had said about him not seeming aggressive. But that sounded crazy, even to Cate as she thought about it.

If Mick were alive, who did they bury?

"When did you say you saw Mick at Lorraine's?" Cate asked.

"Um, hmm," Pal replied, sloshing coffee around in his cup and spilling some onto the front of his coat.

"Mick Brady," Cate tried. "When did you see him at Lorraine's?"

"Oh, yeah," Pal mattered, rocking back-and-forth like he had done yesterday.

Cate began to get frustrated and angry. Apparently, Pal would lock up when anyone asked questions. And that wasn't helpful. Cate turned her body around towards him and put both of her hands on his arm. She wanted to anchor him. To bring his focus to the present moment.

"Pal," she began. "If you really saw my husband at Lorraine's yesterday as you said, and if you know something about his... death, I need to hear about it."

"Um, hmm," Pal muttered again, rocking back-and-forth even harder.

"I'm his wife," Cate tried. "We have three children. Do you realize how serious this is?"

"Yes, ma'am, Mick Brady," Pal muttered. Then his speech became completely incoherent. Cate couldn't tell if it was an act. For all she knew, he might have been perfectly sane and pretending to be deranged. She wasn't qualified to make that judgment. She thought it was odd how Pal had sounded lucid when he first saw her, when he wanted the coffee and sandwich. Maybe that was all he wanted, and he had no interest in other discussions.

What Cate knew, was that she would not get any more information out of the pitiful man. At least not today. With her own self-preservation in mind, she said goodbye to Pal, got up, and walked away.

17

As Cate opened the door and stepped into the chic lobby of Vine Country Magazine, Anna Isley was in her usual spot at the reception desk, smiling, albeit reluctantly.

"Good morning, Cate," Anna said. Cate was distracted, her good vibes ruined by her conversation with Pal.

"Hello, Anna," Cate replied. She wasn't in the mood to chat, so she made a beeline for the elevators. Anna stopped Cate as she walked past.

"I'm sorry," Anna said. She could read Cate's face. "But there's someone here to see you again this morning."

"Detective Fredericks?" Cate asked, a mix of wariness and excitement in her voice.

"No," Anna replied. "It's Nancy DeAngelo. I put her in the conference room and gave her a bottle of water. She's waiting there now."

Cate's eyes nearly popped out of her head she opened

them so wide with surprise. "*Nancy DeAngelo?*" she asked, to clarify. "What does that old witch want?"

Anna nodded, then giggled. She couldn't help herself.

"Thank you, Anna," Cate said. "I appreciate the way you take care of us. I'll handle it from here."

After everything Cate had been through, she didn't think she had an ounce of compassion left for Nancy and her nasty ways. Cate marched directly into the conference room. There was no stopping at the bathroom to freshen her makeup like she did yesterday when she had heard Neil was waiting on her. There was no need for any of that. Cate's objective was to get Nancy out of her office building as quickly as possible. Cate pushed the door open hard as she entered the room. She couldn't tell for sure, but she thought it had made Nancy jump. She hoped it had.

"Hello, Nancy," Cate said, sitting down at the conference table near her mother-in-law. Her voice was cold. She could hear it coming out, but she didn't much care to do anything to change it.

"Hello, Cate," Nancy said, her voice even colder than her daughter-in-law's. Nancy was wearing a black pants suit and looked like she had somewhere formal to go today. It was different from her usual, although not by much.

Cate began to wonder if she would need to get one of the magazine's security officers to escort Nancy out of the building. Cate was more than willing to do so if Nancy wouldn't go quietly. She didn't mind if it made a scene.

"What brings you back to Rosemary Run?" Cate

asked. It was odd for the old woman to be here, all the way from Oklahoma.

"I have a business matter I need to discuss," Nancy said. "Since you are the mother of my grandchildren, I thought I'd give you the courtesy of doing it in person."

Cate scoffed when she heard this. She wasn't sure when Nancy had afforded her any courtesies in the past. She wondered why she would start now. "Okay," Cate said. "What is it?"

"I'll get right down to business," Nancy began. "I have in my possession promissory notes and other financial records which prove that I loaned a substantial amount of money to Mick. I've decided that I want to be paid back for the debt he owed me. I've hired an attorney and I know my rights."

Cate winced as Nancy said the words. "This again? Are you serious?" she asked. "I'm telling you, we had savings. The down payment on our house came directly from our savings. I saw it with my own eyes. I think you're off base here."

"You're sorely mistaken," Nancy said, leaning forward in her chair.

The pair of them looked at each other, locked in disagreement.

"If you have these records like you claim, then let me see them," Cate said.

"Gladly," Nancy replied with an antagonizing smile. She reached into her bag and pulled out a manila file folder. The contents were situated neatly inside. The level of organization made Cate nervous. It made her think perhaps Nancy really did have an attorney involved. Cate still couldn't wrap her mind around the idea that Mick had borrowed money from his mother. He was the one who had wanted to cut her out of their lives. He was the one who didn't want her influencing their children. "It's all there," Nancy said. "See for yourself."

Cate opened the folder to find an itemized summary of payments which had been given to Mick by Nancy. The list was long, but the number of payments wasn't the most alarming part. The dollar amounts nearly made Cate faint, right there in her chair in the conference room.

The total debt, printed in big black letters at the bottom of the page, read 5.3 million dollars. The pages which followed were original promissory notes, complete with Mick's signature. It was his handwriting. Cate was sure of it. And then, at the back of the folder, were bank records showing transfers from Nancy's account at Bank of North America to one in Mick's name at Bay Valley Federal Credit Union. Cate's stomach turned as she saw the records. She and Mick banked at that credit union. If Nancy had been cut out of the Bradys' lives as Mick had claimed was the case, Nancy would not have known where they banked.

"I don't know what to say," Cate stammered. "I certainly didn't know Mick had borrowed any money, let alone this much. Honestly, Nancy, I didn't even know you had this much money."

Cate's mother-in-law was enjoying watching her squirm. "I have this and more, inherited from my father. Just because I'm not showy with it doesn't mean I'm poor. I'm not like your pitiful, blue-collar family."

The words cut Cate like a knife. This was exactly what Nancy did that Cate hated so much. She'd manipulate things to have the upper hand, but she was sneaky about it. She'd act nicer when she needed to get you right where she wanted so she was in control. Cate felt sick at the thought of being indebted to this woman. Five million dollars was a lot of money. More than Cate had ever seen. It was more than she'd probably ever see in her lifetime. She was suddenly furious with Mick for leaving her in this situation. She began to think about the fact that maybe she really would lose the house and have to start over with the kids. Cate didn't know how the courts would treat a debt of this type left for a surviving spouse. She felt helpless to do anything about the situation. And the way things were piling on, Cate didn't know how she would find the strength to tackle one more issue, especially of this magnitude.

"And now you know," Nancy said smugly, pushing the folder further towards Cate. "It's right here, in front of your face. Maybe you should have thought twice about your attitude towards me all these years. From where I'm sitting, it looks like you made a serious mistake in keeping those kids away from me. And now you'll have to pay, literally," Nancy said with an evil laugh. She pointed her finger in Cate's face. "I intend to take every single cent from you that the courts will allow. Find another place to live because I'm coming for that picture-perfect house of yours. You'll be hearing from my attorney."

Nancy picked up the Manila folder from the table, placed it in her bag, and then stomped out of the room, letting the door slam behind her. Cate was left speechless and feeling like she had been punched in the gut. She put her head into her hands and began to cry.

18

"Cate?" Anna asked tentatively as she poked her head in the door to the conference room. She could tell Cate was upset, and she hated to complicate matters any further. Anna wished that she could do something to help Cate. Something to take away the stress and strain.

"Yes?" Cate said, doing her best to sound put together.

"Two things, actually," Anna said. "First, you have a phone call from a Sean O'Brien. He's holding on line one and says he has something urgent to tell you."

Cate pulled her mobile phone out of the pocket of her sweater and looked down at it. She had missed two calls from Sean during the time she'd been with Nancy. She thought maybe he wanted to talk about whatever it was he was trying to tell her this morning, but Cate wasn't terribly interested in that. Cate had a lot else on her mind. She couldn't imagine what it might be that would be as important as he claimed. She suspected Sean had too much time on his hands as a retiree and that he probably just wanted an excuse to chat. It occurred to her, however, that Sean might be calling about Meesha again. Cate decided she had better not ignore him, in case the family dog was in peril.

"Okay," Cate said. "I'll take it in here. Thank you, Anna."

"You're welcome, but when you're finished with that phone call, there is the other thing I mentioned," Anna said, wrinkling up her nose as if she really didn't want to have to say it. She seemed to genuinely hate being the bearer of bad news.

"What?" Cate asked.

"Well, there's a detective here again. He's waiting in the lobby."

"Detective Fredericks?" Cate asked, the enthusiasm obvious in her voice. She could feel her eyes light up and her body tingle when she thought about Neil.

"No, I'm sorry," Anna said. "This is a different detective. He said his name is Luke Hemming."

19

"Sean, what is it?" Cate asked impatiently as she picked up the phone in the conference room and pushed the button for line one. "Is Meesha okay?"

"Oh, hi, Cate," he replied. "As far as I know, Meesha is fine. She's at your house, right?"

"She was when I left her about an hour ago," Cate said. "I just thought…"

"Yeah, that's not why I'm calling," Sean clarified.

"What is it then?"

"I guess I'll just come right out and say it," Sean mumbled, sounding awkward. "I saw something I think you need to know about."

This again, Cate thought.

"Sean," Cate said. "I'm in a hurry today. I have someone waiting for me as we speak. I don't mean to be short, but can we talk about this tonight when I get home? Because if it's about what the police asked you…"

"It's more than that. It's… I think it's pretty important," he replied. "I think I should tell the police, but

I wanted to make sure it was okay with you first since it concerns your family."

Sean had Cate's full attention now.

"Go on," she said.

"You want me to tell you now? Or tonight?"

Cate was growing weary of Sean's sluggishness. He was a nice man. She knew she was being unreasonable, but she couldn't seem to help being short with him today.

"Yes, we'll do it now," she blurted. "What?"

Sean hesitated. Collecting his thoughts. "Is this phone line monitored?"

"Why do you ask?"

"It's… oh, nevermind. I'll go ahead," he conceded. "It's about last night's break-in at your house."

"Okay," Cate said as she waited for Sean to spit it out. She wondered what this could have to do with her family, other than her family's safety at their home.

"I saw someone." There was silence on the line as Cate waited. "Two people, actually. A man and a woman. They were driving down our street last night, past my house. And away from yours. Not long before I discovered Meesha roaming around."

"Okay," Cate said, interested now.

"It was getting dark, and the storm was picking up. Mitchell and I were in our front room looking for candles in preparation for what I assumed would be an inevitable power outage. I looked out the window and saw that wind gusts were blowing things around all over the place. When I noticed the car go by, I remember thinking it was odd for them to be out in that weather. It seemed like they should have been hunkering down indoors, you know?"

"Yes," Cate said, nodding, even though no one was there to see it.

"I didn't get a look at the man's face, but the woman…" Sean's voice trailed off.

"Go on," Cate prompted.

"I didn't recognize her at first. That's why I didn't mention it when I called to tell you about Meesha or when I called back about your front door being wide open. But while lying in bed last night, it dawned on me that I knew who she was."

"Who was it?" Cate asked, exasperated. She thought Sean might never get to the point.

"I haven't said anything to the police yet." He took a deep breath before he spoke the woman's name, nervous about saying what he knew. "I'm pretty sure it was your mother-in-law. Nancy, right? From Oklahoma? I remember meeting her the day of the funeral."

"Oh," Cate replied. She now knew Nancy was in town, but she was surprised to hear that her mother-in-law and a male companion were on her street last night. "Yeah, she's in town. She showed up unexpectedly. I was actually with her when you called. She just left my office building."

"Did you know she had been at your house?"

"No, but I guess it makes sense. She and her husband Al must have stopped by when we weren't home," Cate explained. She wasn't sure what to make of this new information. It sounded harmless, like Nancy and Al had simply stopped by to see the kids. Or maybe Nancy had wanted to deliver her manila folder to Cate last night instead of this morning.

"The man with her wasn't her husband," Sean said, sounding very sure.

"Wait. What?" Cate asked. "Who else would it have been if not Al?"

"I don't know, but the man I saw was younger than Al. He was fit and muscular. No offense to your father-in-law, but there's no way it was him. I got a good look at the man's midsection."

"And you think they were coming from my house?"

"I can't say for certain," Sean replied. "But it sure looked that way. They were going slowly when I first saw them on Flock Hollow Lane as if they had just turned onto our street from the access point to the alley behind our homes. They sped up quickly as they passed by."

"And you're sure it was Nancy?"

"Yeah, I am."

20

"Mrs. Cate Brady," Detective Hemming said as he stood up to shake Cate's hand. "I'm Detective Luke Hemming from the Rosemary Run Police Department." He looked and sounded serious. He didn't seem to care that the lobby was bustling with people. He wasn't friendly like Neil had been.

"Hello," Cate said in return. "What can I do for you today, Detective Hemming?"

Luke was a new detective who had moved to the area from Reno earlier this year. Cate had heard his name, but hadn't met him in person until now. He was a handsome African-American man with strong features and an athletic build. He wasn't an eligible bachelor like Neil Frederick though. Cate had heard that Luke had a wife and a young family. If she was remembering correctly, Luke's twin daughters attended Niko's preschool.

"I'll skip the niceties," he said. "Mrs. Brady, I'd like you to come down to the station and answer some questions for me."

Cate's face flushed as the reality of what she knew was coming began to unfold. "Am I under arrest, Detective Hemming?" she asked.

"Not yet," he replied, stoically. "At this time, we request your voluntary cooperation."

"So, I'm not *required* to come to the station right now?" Cate asked. She was impressed with herself at keeping a level head in this tense situation, especially given everything else on her mind.

"That's right." Luke shifted his weight and lowered one eyebrow as he looked hard at Cate. "Do you have something to hide, Mrs. Brady?"

People in the lobby were beginning to notice now. Cate could see Anna out of the corner of her eye, looking concerned and wringing her hands behind the reception desk. Luke wasn't talking loudly, but it was as if everyone in the vicinity was picking up on his powerful body language.

"No, of course not," Cate said, in a quieter voice. "I'm simply asking so I understand my rights."

Luke kept eye contact with Cate, but didn't say anything else. He had a confidence about him she admired and respected. She could tell he was a good cop. Rosemary Run was lucky to have him.

"Does my brother know about this?" Cate asked.

Luke didn't blink. And he didn't answer the question. Cate didn't dare ask if Neil knew. She realized that keeping what had happened between them quiet was in both of their best interests. She stood quietly for a moment, tapping one finger on the inseam of her pants and considering whether to cooperate. She wondered if this was the best time to consult an attorney. She thought perhaps it wasn't necessary. Maybe Luke was conducting a fishing expedition to see what Cate had to say. She supposed it wouldn't hurt to go on down to the station and hear them out. Perhaps she could learn something that would turn out to be useful.

"Fine," Cate said. "I'd be happy to come down to the station and answer your questions, Detective Hemming. Shall we do that now?"

"Yes," Luke said. He was keeping things so formal that he didn't even bother to use more than one-word answers. He nodded his thanks.

"I'll tell my boss I'm leaving and I'll meet you there," Cate said.

Luke nodded again, then turned and walked out the front door.

21

Cate stopped at the bathroom on the way upstairs. It was empty, so she went into the same stall she had the morning before, hoping maybe she could cry a little. She thought it might help her to get out some of the emotions which felt like they were about to bubble over the surface. Only this time, no tears would come. Cate felt frozen in time, like an animal in headlights whose flight or fight response hadn't kicked in yet. She was thankful that her mind and her mouth had worked well enough to speak to Luke appropriately, but she could tell her body was in shock. Not knowing what else to do, she pulled her mobile phone out of her pocket and dialed her parents.

"Cate Bear!" Ron said, after picking up on the first ring. He hadn't called her Cate Bear in a long time, but was doing it frequently over the past couple of days. Cate thought it odd, but she didn't mind. Right now, she needed all the love and support from her parents she could get. "How are you, Kid?"

"I'm okay, Daddy," Cate said, her voice shaky. "Did

you and Mom get the goats back safely last night? And are you getting the barn repaired?"

"Yes, Fred and Ginger are fine. Safe and sound. We have someone coming to patch up the barn tomorrow. But what's wrong?" Ron asked, the concern evident in his voice.

Cate knew she could get right down to it. There was no reason to beat around the bush with her parents. "The police have asked me to come in and answer some questions for them. They're investigating Mick's death. They think it might not have been an accident and they suspect I may have been involved."

"What in the world?" Ron asked rhetorically. "That's the most ridiculous thing I've ever heard. Oh, my darling girl. I'm so sorry."

That did it. The tears began to flow freely. "Daddy, I don't know what to do," Cate said as she sobbed. "I knew this was coming, believe it or not. There's a lot I haven't had a chance to tell you and Mom. But now that it's happening, I feel like someone has put a bolt of lightning into my body. I'm all amped up and frozen at the same time. I'm not sure I can make any sense when they question me."

"You'll do fine, Cate Bear," Ron reassured. "You have nothing to hide. Just try and relax and be yourself."

Cate nodded silently. She could hear her mom in the distance asking what was going on, then she heard her dad cover the phone with his hand and mutter a few key words to Ellen. "Honey," he said to his daughter when he returned. "Are you going right now?"

"Yes," Cate said. "I just need to tell Laura that I'm

leaving. I hope she doesn't get too upset with me. I've missed so much work lately and now, two mornings in a row, police officers have waited for me in the lobby."

"No need to say another word," Ron replied. "Your mom and I are coming up there. We'll meet you at the station."

As Cate hung up the phone, she felt relieved. She thought it was perhaps juvenile and immature to have called her parents, but she needed them now more than ever. She dried her tears and pulled herself together, then went upstairs to gather her things and speak with her boss. Luckily, Laura was gracious and didn't seem to mind the additional ask. She reassured Cate that she had known her return to work after her husband's sudden death would be a bumpy road. She said that Vine Country Magazine would be there waiting with open arms when Cate was ready to return to a more normal schedule.

Appreciative, Cate headed back downstairs and past the reception desk. Anna Isley could tell that Cate had been crying. She stepped out from around the desk as Cate walked past and she wrapped her arm around Cate's shoulders. "If there's anything I can do…" Anna said.

"I know," Cate replied. "Thank you."

Sasha hadn't arrived yet this morning, but Cate asked Anna to please tell her friend what had happened when she got there.

As Cate walked out the front door of her office building and stepped into the pleasant October day, she thought how sad it was that all of her happy thoughts had come crashing down around her in such a short time. Although part of her had known it would happen that way. Maybe she had wanted to squeeze every bit of happiness out that she still could.

Pal wasn't on his usual spot on the bench as Cate walked by. She thought it was strange, but then again, she was usually in her office building this time of morning and wasn't sure what his typical patterns were. For all she knew, he spent some of the day out of the direct sun when it wasn't mealtime. Cate walked on without thinking too much about it. She continued to the parking garage, where she got in her SUV and drove towards the police station.

By the time she arrived, Luke had a chair ready for her at a table in an interrogation room. He waved her in and she could see that Neil was waiting inside the room. She looked around nervously for her parents. She felt like a jumbled mess, feeling both excited by the prospect of seeing the man she had made love to last night and wanting her parents to be with her during the interview. She thought about how a grown woman wouldn't need her parents. And a child wouldn't have had any business making love to a handsome police officer. Cate wasn't sure what she was anymore.

Just in time, Ron and Ellen burst through the front doors of the station, looking every bit the part of protective parents.

"My mom and dad are here," Cate said to Luke. "Can they join me?"

Luke glanced over at Neil, who shrugged his shoulders and nodded his head. "It's not exactly typical for a woman of your age to bring her parents when she comes in for questioning," Luke said. "But I suppose there's no harm in it at this juncture. They must remain quiet and listen only."

"Thank you," Cate said gratefully. "I understand. They'll be quiet." She turned back towards her parents and motioned for them to follow her.

Neil looked down at the floor as everyone piled into the interrogation room. Cate could see there were cameras set up to record everything that happened. She knew Neil was probably being careful to avoid having the cameras pick up on the budding relationship between the two of them. She knew they would need to stick to business. They would have to avoid pleasantries and affectionate glances.

"Everyone," Luke began. "I'm Detective Luke Hemming and this is my associate, Detective Neil Fredericks. Cate, I believe you're now acquainted with us both?"

"Yes, I am," Cate said. She turned towards her parents, who were getting themselves situated in chairs which a young officer had brought into the back of the room for them. "These are my parents, Ron and Ellen Tatum."

"Officer James Tatum is our son," Ron added as he reached out to shake Luke's hand. "My wife and I appreciate the good work you folks do here."

"Thank you, Mr. Tatum," Luke said. Cate thought Luke's tone sounded much friendlier with her dad than it had when he was speaking with her. "As I explained to your daughter, it's okay for you and your wife to be here and to listen, but we need you to remain silent. Understood?"

"Yes, certainly," Ron replied.

"We wouldn't want to get in the way," Ellen said, affirming her husband's position.

"Good," Luke replied. "Now, with that settled, Cate, do we have your permission to record this conversation? It's not required at this time and you can say no, but the recording will help us as we review the case. It might even prevent us from having to question you a second time in the event we need clarification on something."

Cate looked at Neil for guidance, but quickly remembered that she shouldn't do so. Instead, she turned to her parents and asked them with her eyes what they thought. Both Ron and Ellen nodded, so Cate turned back to Luke and gave her permission.

"Good," he said as he connected the video recorder. A red light turned on and began to blink. Even though the light was tiny, Cate suddenly felt its assault on her state of mind. She wondered if that was part of the plan. She imagined a blinking red light might drive a guilty person to confess if they had to endure too many hours of it during heated questioning. It made Cate think of Chinese water torture and how small irritations could become maddening over enough time.

Cate sat down in the chair Luke had set out for her. Luke sat on the other side of the table and Neil pulled his chair over from the corner and re-positioned himself beside his partner. Cate felt outnumbered. She wondered if that was part of the plan.

"Mrs. Brady," Luke began. "Detective Fredericks and I will ask you a series of questions related to your husband Mick Brady's death. You are not obligated to answer our questions at this time, but we appreciate your cooperation in doing so."

"I'm entitled to an attorney if I want one, correct?" Cate asked, to confirm.

"Yes, that's right," Luke replied. "If it any point during this interview you decide you'd like to have an attorney present, we will stop where we are until such time that your attorney can join you."

"And if I cannot afford an attorney, one will be appointed for me?" Cate asked, thinking about Nancy and the five million dollar balance that Mick owed her. Cate could hear Ron and Ellen squirming. But they had promised to remain silent and were following instructions.

"That's only if you're under arrest, Mrs. Brady," Luke said. "Do you anticipate being placed under arrest?"

Cate fiddled with one of the buttons on her sweater. "No, of course not," Cate said, remembering that she had spoken those exact same words earlier when Luke had asked if she had anything to hide. She thought she had better vary her responses a bit or it might sound suspicious. "I mean... I certainly hope not. I don't know of any reason I would be arrested," she tried. He didn't look up, but Cate could tell that Neil felt bad for her. His brow was furrowed and his shoulders looked tense.

"Let's begin with a repeat of one of the questions Detective Fredericks asked you yesterday," Luke said. "Where were you the night your husband was killed?"

"I told all of this to Neil... to Detective Fredericks yesterday when he asked," Cate said, correcting herself mid-sentence. For the first time since Cate had arrived at the police station, Neil looked up and made eye contact with her. It seemed like he couldn't help himself. He looked back down right away, but in that split-second, they had made a connection. Cate felt a warm rush spread across her body. She was beginning to realize that she really was interested in Neil Fredericks. She hoped what they had would turn out to be more than a fling.

"Humor us," Luke said, his tone flat. "Let's go over it again."

Cate responded the same as she had to Neil the day before. She explained how Jilly and Aaron had ridden home with friends from the neighborhood that day and were at the house waiting when she and Niko arrived. She told the detective how she had been making homemade pizza with the kids when James had knocked on the door to tell her the bad news.

"What time did you leave work that day, Mrs. Brady?" Luke asked.

"I don't remember exactly, but I usually leave around four."

"And you told Detective Fredericks that you arrived home that day sometime around five PM, correct?" Luke asked. Cate could tell he was trying to trip her up.

"I believe so, yes. I wasn't paying very close attention as it was happening. It was just an ordinary day until… We got the news."

"Mrs. Brady, how many miles is it from your office to your son Niko Brady's preschool?"

Cate could see what Luke was getting at and she didn't like it. The thought of having her every step traced made her uneasy. "I don't know for sure," she said. "I've never measured it."

"Well, I have," Luke said. Neil's shoulders seemed to tense up even further in response to this statement. "It's 3.4 miles away. Does that sound accurate?"

"Sure, I suppose," Cate said.

"And how about the distance between Niko Brady's preschool and your home on Flock Hollow Lane?"

Luke's line of questioning was becoming painful for everyone in the room. He could have come out and just said that he thought it had taken Cate too long to get home that day. She wished he would avoid the theatrics and settle down to the point.

"I'm not sure about that either," Cate said. "But it's less than ten miles."

"You're right," Luke said. "It's 8.7 miles. So 3.4 miles plus 8.7 miles, figuring in a little traffic and time to walk inside and check Niko out. Sound about right?"

"Yeah, I guess so," Cate replied.

"By my estimate, that should have taken about half an hour. Yet, you claimed it took an hour. How do you explain that?"

"I don't know," Cate replied. "Aren't we splitting hairs here? As I said, I wasn't looking at the clock or checking the exact time. I didn't do it that day because I don't do it any day. Sometimes I leave work a little later than four. Some days, traffic is thicker than others. Sometimes it takes longer to get in and out of the preschool. There are numerous factors which could easily skew my estimate."

"Huh," Luke groaned. "Interesting." Neil looked at Luke and visibly winced. It was his turn and he didn't want to go through with it. "Over to you," Luke said to his partner.

Neil had no choice. He had to question her. "Mrs. Brady," Neil said, looking up again, reluctantly. It pained Cate to hear him addressing her so formally again. She thought back to their conversation at her house last night when he had asked about her maiden name. She wished he would call her Cate. It felt wrong to pretend that the two of them didn't care for each other.

"Yes?" Cate said, trying her best to sound casual.

"I'll get to the point," Neil said. "We've spoken with someone in the accounting department of Vine Country Magazine who claims to have seen you leaving the office that day at 3:30 PM. The record at your son's preschool shows him being signed out at 4:55. That leaves approximately an hour and a half not accounted for. Can you explain that to us?" Neil looked almost sick as he asked Cate this question. Cate had thought he was on her side, especially after last night. But she didn't like where this was headed.

"That's simply not true," Cate said. "I was at work later that day. I'm sure of it. Maybe the person in the accounting department saw me heading out to get an afternoon tea, as I sometimes do. I don't know what they saw. But I know I didn't leave work any earlier than usual."

"How can you be so certain?" Neil asked. "Do you remember specifically what you did that afternoon?"

"Yes," Cate replied. "I was making plans to go visit the new winery that opened recently by the bay-- Valley Vineyards. I'm writing a feature article about the new business that will be published early next summer, just in time for the peak tourist season. That afternoon, I was at my desk, reading over the winery's website on the Internet and taking notes."

"We will need to verify that and to look at some timestamps," Neil said. "Were you using your laptop or your desktop computer?"

"I was using my laptop," Cate said.

"Forgive me, but that seems odd," Neil remarked. "If you were at your desk in your office, wouldn't you have been using your desktop computer? It has a larger screen and a more powerful processor. Internet browsing would have been faster on the desktop."

"It's not odd at all," Cate replied, getting frustrated. "I often use my laptop in my office because, when doing so, I can situate myself to get a great view of the hills out my window. The cord for the desktop computer isn't long enough to reach, but with my laptop, I can enjoy the beautiful Rosemary Run natural scenery out in the distance. Ask my colleagues. They'll tell you I do it all the time."

Neil took a deep breath to prepare himself for what he had to say next. "Mrs. Brady, were you aware that you are the beneficiary of an unusually large life insurance policy in your husband's name?"

"No, I wasn't," she said. "I knew he'd receive a death benefit from the Navy, but I wasn't aware of anything else. I've been meaning to check on that, but haven't gotten around to it."

"Do you have any idea how much the policy is for?" Neil asked.

"No," Cate confirmed. "I told you. I wasn't aware of any policy, so I don't know how much it was for."

"Over five million dollars," Neil said. "5.5 million, to be exact." Cate's eyes grew wide as she heard the number and thought about the amount of the debt to Nancy. It probably wasn't any coincidence that the life insurance policy Mick had taken out was just enough to cover his debt and to leave a few hundred thousand for the family. With such a payout, their home would be secure and they would have enough cushion to continue living a normal life.

"You look surprised?" Neil asked. "Is this making sense to you somehow?"

Cate turned around in her chair and looked at her parents as if she were silently requesting their emotional support. She wasn't sure whether she should tell the police about Nancy and the promissory note or about Sean claiming to see Nancy driving away from her house around the time of the break-in last night. She wasn't sure how much Neil had shared with Luke about what she had told him. And she wasn't sure if James had made any progress looking into the matters she had asked him about. Cate needed to decide quickly. Luke was watching her like a hawk and recording her every move on video.

"No," Cate said. "That's just a really large number. That's more money than I've ever seen in my life. I don't understand why Mick would hide something like that from me."

"And that's the first thing you've said today I'm certain I believe," Luke muttered. Neil gave him a dirty look, expressing his disdain for his partner's treatment of Cate. But they weren't done yet. Neil had to ask her one more pointed question.

"Mrs. Brady," he began. "Do you know how your husband died?"

Cate took a breath before answering. It saddened her to think about her husband's demise. "I only know that he had an accident and was pronounced dead on the scene," Cate said. "Like I told you before, Detective Fredericks, I don't know the details. And frankly, I'm not sure I need to know the details. I'm not the type who wants to know the nitty-gritty. I'd rather remember Mick the way he was, healthy and vibrant. Besides, knowing exactly what happened will not bring my husband back."

Neil looked at Luke, who pushed pause on the video recording device and turned to Cate. "That'll be all for now, Mrs. Brady. Enjoy this beautiful day."

I n the days that followed, as October crept closer and closer towards November, things were blessedly quiet. Cate got her house cleaned up and went down to three-quarters time at work to ensure she'd have time to see that her kids enjoyed the upcoming holidays. Her boss was supportive. Cate had gotten into the habit of working at the office in the morning and then leaving around lunchtime to come home and do a few more hours from there. Much of what Cate did for the magazine was solitary anyway, so working from home had been an easy transition. In fact, Cate found that she could often be more productive at home since there weren't any distractions. She was producing the same amount of content in three-quarters time as she had previously at full time in the office. Cate wished she had suggested the flex schedule from the beginning. It would have afforded her more time to spend with Mick before he died.

Cate had expected to receive communication from Nancy or her attorneys by now, but, so far, she hadn't heard anything. She thought, just maybe, Nancy had decided to give up on pursuing Cate for the collection of Mick's debt. Apparently, Nancy had inherited a lot more money than Cate ever realized. Perhaps Nancy had decided that she had enough riches left in her coffers and should allow Cate and the kids to remain in the house they called home. Cate knew that was unlikely, but it was nice to dream about.

The police department had left Cate alone for the past few days. And, as far as she knew, Cate hadn't been followed by a man in a dark-colored sedan. She was feeling a little safer again. She and the kids had spent most of their free time decorating the house for Halloween and preparing costumes.

Aaron had decided to dress like a punk rocker with one of Mick's old Rolling Stones T-shirts and a headband that made it look like he had a bright red mohawk. The young teenager planned to keep a guitar around his neck to complete the look. Jilly had chosen to make a scarecrow costume. She had found some old overalls and a flannel shirt at a secondhand store, which she planned to stuff with straw from Ron and Ellen's farm. She would divide her hair into two sections and braid each side, then she'd use makeup to place large freckles on her cheeks and to draw exaggerated pink lips. The whole look would be topped with a wide-brimmed straw hat. Niko wanted to be a lion, so Cate was helping him get his costume together. She had found a pattern online and was sewing him a hood with loose loops of orange yarn strategically placed to look like a mane. Cate had purchased her young son a tan turtleneck and pants to match. To complete the look, she would pin a felt tail to his little bottom.

The kids were all excited. Cate thought it would be great. It wouldn't be the same without Mick, but Cate was determined to make Halloween as good as it could possibly be. She thought she was on the right track. She knew more trouble was coming. But she was doing her best to enjoy the calm before the next storm.

As for Neil Fredericks, Cate had seen him twice more. They were trying to give it space, but were having a hard time staying away from each other. The evening after Cate had gone into the police station to answer their questions, she ended up at Neil's house. It had been early evening, just before Cate had gone to get the kids from James and Rebecca's. She had been driving around town, trying to make sense out of everything that was happening, when she called Neil's mobile phone and find out what he was doing. He invited her over. She accepted, thinking they would just talk for a few minutes. When she arrived and Neil closed his heavy, wooden door behind her, they lasted less than a minute before they buried themselves in each other's arms and made love in Neil's bed. The same thing had happened two days later when Cate called Neil at lunchtime after leaving the office for the day. He was at his house for lunch and he invited Cate over again. That day, Cate had taken off her wedding ring and secured it in a zipper pouch in the back of her purse. Despite plans to just talk, Cate and Neil couldn't keep their hands off of each other and, once again, made passionate love in Neil's bed.

When she was with him, Cate didn't care what anyone

thought or what consequences might come from having a relationship with a detective who was investigating her as part of a murder case. Her problems seemed to fade into the distance when Neil was by her side. Cate knew things couldn't go on this way for long. Eventually someone would find out that she and Neil were seeing each other and word would spread around town. They would reach a point where they'd have to decide whether to pursue a real relationship and go public with it or to end things.

Cate had spent a lot of time imagining what a real relationship with Neil might look like. She had told herself that, although she never expected to fall in love a week after her husband died, it had happened that way, right before her very eyes. She often thought about Mick and about what he would say if he knew. She had been faithful to him all the years they had been together and had never even considered being with anyone else. But Mick was gone now. And Neil seemed to have shown up in Cate's life in a way that she couldn't ignore. She figured if fate intended them to be together, she might as well not fight it. Cate thought Mick would approve and would want her to be happy.

Even though things had gone pretty well for the Brady family for a few days, there was one thing that continued to bug Cate. It was what Pal had said about seeing Mick at Lorraine's Diner. Even though the homeless man had said nothing else which had seemed reasonable or lucid, Cate couldn't get his comment about Lorraine's out of her mind. To make matters worse, James had been dragging his feet on looking into the things he had promised his sister he would check into. She wasn't mad at him. She figured her big brother was doing the best he could, but she wanted to find out more and was willing to do the legwork herself.

On another cool October morning, Cate decided to take matters into her own hands. She saw her kids off to the bus stop and preschool, then took a notion to go down to Lorraine's Diner before work and talk to the owner in person. Whatever Pal had seen, Cate thought perhaps Tim Negly could explain so she could make sense out of it. She drove quickly, exhilarated by the thrill of the hunt.

The dining room was packed when Cate arrived. Lorraine's was an old fifties style diner, and the building was outfitted in shiny silver metal. There were round barstools lining the counter and a row of booths along the wall of windows. A waitress said hello to Cate as she walked in the door and directed her to a booth on the far side of the dining room. Cate hadn't been in Lorraine's since moving back home to Rosemary Run, but she had eaten there all the time as a kid. Lorraine Negley had owned and operated the place for nearly forty years before turning it over to her son, Tim, so she could enjoy her retirement years in Phoenix, Arizona. Cate didn't know Tim other than to recognize his face, but Ron and Ellen had been close friends with Lorraine. Cate hoped that their parents' relationship would help persuade Tim to help her.

As soon as Cate sat down, a pretty Asian waitress named Kai showed up at the table to take her order. Cate wasn't sure what time of day Tim worked, so she didn't know whether he'd be at the diner this morning.

"Hi, good morning," Kai said cheerfully. "What can I get for you, Miss?"

"I'd love a cup of coffee and a Southwest-style omelet," Cate replied with a smile. The thought of Lorraine enjoying retirement down in Arizona made Cate hungry for southwestern food.

"Coming right up," Kai confirmed. She moved fast and had already turned around to head to the kitchen when Cate stopped her.

"Also, if Tim Negley is here this morning, I'd like to talk with him. His mom and my parents are old friends," Cate said.

"You're in luck," Kai announced, turning back again. "Because Tim isn't usually here this time of the morning. But today, he came in early. He's in the office. I will ask him to come out and see you."

"Wonderful," Cate said. She hoped Kai wouldn't feel deceived when there was more to the story than their parents having been old friends. Kai trotted off while Cate made herself comfortable in her seat.

A short time later, Tim Negley himself arrived at Cate's table and sat down across from her. He reached out his hand and introduced himself. "Tim Negley," he said. "I'm Lorraine's son. Kai tells me that our parents knew each other?" He smiled while he talked. Tim seemed like the type who genuinely enjoyed being around people. Cate remembered his mom as having been the same way. She was certain that their shared affinity for relationships was a large part of what had made Lorraine's so popular for so many years.

"Yes, that's right," Cate said. "My mom and dad are Ron and Ellen Tatum."

"Ah, yes," Tim said, with an even bigger smile. "Good people, those two. You must be the daughter that moved away."

"That's me! I'm Cate," she said, careful not to mention her last name yet. "My husband was in the Navy and so we traveled around a lot. We moved back home to Rosemary Run a little more than a year ago... When he retired."

"Glad to hear it," Tim said. "It's always good to have one of our own come back home."

Cate could tell Tim wouldn't be able to stay and chat for long. He was focusing his attention on her, but every now and then his eyes would dart to something happening elsewhere in the diner. He seemed to be fighting the urge to get up and refill drinks and clear dirty plates off the counter. Cate knew she needed to get to the point if she had any hope of learning some real information this morning.

"Tim, there's another reason I came to see you this morning. It goes beyond our parents having known each other. It's something I need to ask you about."

Tim leaned back against the padded booth and placed his arms at his sides with his palms on the seat cushion below him. "Okay, go ahead and ask," he said.

"It's about my husband. Mick Brady." Cate could see Tim's body react when he heard Mick's name. His eyelids twitched and he leaned his chin to one side. She could tell he knew the name.

"I'm sorry. I don't know any Mick Brady. But it's been lovely to meet you, Cate. Now if you'll excuse me..."

"I only need another minute," Cate said. "I know a homeless man named Pal. I don't know his last name, but he hangs around my office building downtown quite a bit and I've taken to buying him breakfast sandwiches and coffee." Tim relaxed in his seat again and looked at Cate as he listened.

"Okay," Tim said. "Would you like to take him some leftovers that haven't been sold by the time we switch over to our lunch menu? If you could swing back by around eleven..."

"No... Well, maybe," Cate replied. "That's a very kind offer that I'm sure Pal and some of the other homeless people downtown would appreciate. But that's not what I came here to ask about." Tim pursed his lips, apparently realizing what was coming. "Pal said something very strange to me the other day," Cate continued. "I haven't been able to get it off my mind."

"And what was that?" Tim asked.

"He said that he'd seen my husband, Mick Brady, talking to you here at the diner less than a week ago. But the thing is, my husband has been dead for nearly two weeks now. Do you have any idea why Pal would say such a thing?"

Tim bristled. "Truly, I'm sorry," he said as he stood up. "I can't help you, Cate. Please tell your parents hello for me. I'll do the same when I talk to my mom. Now, enjoy your breakfast and have a good day." Tim turned and walked away before Cate could stop him. He seemed determined to end their conversation. But Cate wasn't finished yet. Tim's reaction only made her more eager to dig deep. It was obvious there was something Tim Negley wasn't telling her.

Cate stood, leaving her belongings at the table, and followed Tim as he walked towards the kitchen. "Hey, Tim" Cate called out. "I can tell you know more than you're letting on. Please don't leave me in the dark. After the history that our parents had together, can you at least give me that?"

Tim stopped and stood still for a moment, his back to Cate. He was considering what she had asked of him. "Cate, please walk away," he said.

"I'm not going to do that," Cate replied. "This is my husband we're talking about. I see a wedding ring on your finger, Tim. Wouldn't you want answers if it were your wife?"

Reluctantly, Tim moved to face Cate. He pulled her to one side up against the wall and whispered, "Look, Cate Brady, you need to leave this alone. You're out of your depth here. Trust me. Go home and forget we ever had this conversation." Then Tim turned around and walked away, the metal door to the kitchen closing obediently behind him.

23

The next morning, Cate was awakened bright and early by the sound of Meesha barking at the front door. Halloween was just a day away and Cate had been up late the night before putting finishing touches on the kids' costumes. She stumbled out of bed to see what the commotion was about, wiping her bleary eyes as she walked into the living room. She tried to remain calm about Meesha's level of alarm, but was a bit jumpy these days, what with everything that had happened.

To Cate's relief, Meesha was barking at a delivery driver who had placed a neat brown box on the front porch. She knew what was inside the moment she saw the package. The security cameras she ordered had finally arrived.

Cate had spent most of the night tossing and turning, distressed by what had happened at Lorraine's diner. She was becoming more and more driven to find answers. Tim had acted so strangely. His behavior, combined with Pal's comments, made Cate wonder if Mick really could be alive. If he were, she was determined to know about it.

She opened the package and installed the security cameras right away. As it turned out, she didn't need her brother's help to set them up. The instructions were self-explanatory. Cate was able to get them placed and connected before the kids had even woken up and come downstairs for breakfast. She didn't bother to tell them about the cameras, figuring maybe it was better that way. She didn't want them to be afraid in their own home. Cate didn't know exactly what she hoped to capture with the new devices, but if someone was snooping around the house, she wanted to see their face.

She fed the kids breakfast, like usual, and they all headed out to begin their day.

24

Detective Luke Hemming sat at his desk and poured two sugar packets into his coffee, stirring the mixture up with one finger. It was the day before Halloween and he was hoping to bring Cate Brady under arrest before the new month turned. He wanted justice for poor Mick. Luke knew that when someone died and there was any hint of foul play involved, statistically, it was most often the spouse who was the guilty party. He had been a detective long enough to have seen the sinister combo of a life lost too soon and a greedy spouse looking to cash in on a huge insurance policy.

Luke knew that both his partner, Detective Neil Fredericks, and Cate's brother, Officer James Tatum, were on her side. Luke was aware that both men were working behind the scenes to exonerate Cate Brady and to keep her protected.

Detective Fredericks had been on the straight and narrow side of the law in the beginning, but he had quickly become soft due to his budding romantic relationship with the suspect. Neil thought Luke hadn't noticed, but Luke Hemming noticed everything. He saw the gleam in Neil's eyes when he talked about her. He saw the way Neil stood up straighter and puffed his chest out when she was in the room. And he saw the way her car had been repeatedly parked in Neil's driveway for an hour or so at a time during their personal visits.

What Detective Fredericks and Officer Tatum didn't know was that Luke had done his homework. It had taken some digging, but he had found it, just as he suspected he would. Cate Brady had a record. One which painted her in the light of a cold-blooded murderer.

25

C ate's morning again looked like it was shaping up to be a good one. She made an effort to appreciate the little things in each moment, as was her new practice now that she knew her life could crash down into pieces without warning. When she arrived downtown, Pal was there and, as usual, she bought two cups of coffee and two breakfast sandwiches from the Brick House Cafe to share. Pal seemed dissociated again, so she handed him the food and coffee, then went on into her office building without attempting to initiate discussion. She walked by the reception desk and greeted Anna, making a joke about how, luckily, no police officers were waiting to question her this morning. She stopped by her friend Sasha's office to chat for a while and then settled in at her desk for what she hoped would be a productive morning's work. Only when she opened up her bag to pull out her laptop, it wasn't there.

Damn it, Cate thought to herself.

She knew she must have forgotten it at home. She had

been distracted by setting up the security cameras. As she thought back and retraced her steps, she remembered that the laptop had been left sitting on the kitchen counter. All the files Cate needed to work on this morning were stored locally on her laptop and were not backed up to the cloud. Annoyed, Cate knew she would have to return home and retrieve the laptop if she were going to get anything accomplished that day.

She gathered her things and walked back downstairs, back past Anna, and back out to the parking garage. She got into her SUV and drove home, thinking to herself how that laptop was causing her trouble. Cate began to consider that perhaps she should change the way she managed her digital files. At a minimum, a cloud backup would have prevented her from having to go back home this morning. Her house wasn't far from her office, but it felt like wasted time to return there when she had left it only an hour before. Not to mention, Neil seemed to have focused on her laptop when he was questioning her at the police station. She thought it silly. They hadn't discussed it when they'd seen each other afterward because the two of them had decided not to talk about the investigation when they were together. But it had sounded at the station like Cate's use of her laptop instead of her desktop on the afternoon Mick died incited suspicion.

When Cate walked in the front door of her house, the laptop was there on the counter just like she had remembered, nestled amongst bags of Halloween candy to be handed out to trick-or-treaters. The back door was slightly ajar, too. Cate thought it odd and began to feel afraid, but could explain the open door once she jogged her memory again. Jilly had been last out that door this morning on her way to the bus stop. Cate and Niko had been home awhile longer, then had gone out the front. Knowing how Jilly sometimes forgets to latch doors in favor of letting them swing closed behind her, Cate told herself that everything was probably fine. Her daughter had known she would not be the last one out of the house, so Cate couldn't blame her for not double-checking. Cate made a mental note to latch and lock all the doors herself before leaving the house each morning. Out of an abundance of caution, she looked around the house to be sure everything was okay. She found that all was quiet. Nothing seemed to be out of place.

Satisfied nothing was wrong, Cate took a few minutes to use her own bathroom while she was home. When she finished, she checked her hair in the framed bedroom mirror above her large wooden dresser. She loved the farmhouse-style furniture she and Mick had picked out for their bedroom. Cate's thoughts drifted to Neil and how it would be strange to make love to him in the bed she had shared with her husband. For now, she'd avoid that discomfort by sleeping with him at his house only. Maybe, she thought, when she was ready, she'd purchase a new bedroom set to start fresh. If Nancy didn't take her house and all of her money away first.

As she returned to the kitchen and began to pack up her laptop computer, Cate took a notion to check the security camera footage. She didn't expect it to have captured anything since she had only been gone a short while. But she was excited to have the devices up and running and was feeling especially proud that she'd been able to complete the setup process all by herself. She knew that checking the footage would become a routine, so she figured she might as well start now. She sat down, opened the laptop, and cued up the feed.

At first, there was nothing to see. Just the empty house with no movement, save for Meesha lumbering around from one resting spot to another. Thinking this might take a few minutes, Cate hit fast forward on the feed and stood up to get herself a glass of water. She filled her glass with ice and was watching the footage out of the corner of her eye as she held it under the tap. Then Cate saw something. It was a male figure, walking in the back door of her home casually as if he owned the place. Meesha could be seen on tape sauntering up to greet the man while wagging her tail.

Cate's heart lurched inside her chest and she thought she might throw up. She dropped the glass onto the floor, where it shattered into pieces with a thud. She knew that figure. Even though she was seeing the footage on fast forward, Cate recognized the way he carried himself. She *remembered* that man. She remembered his movements, his posture, and his body language. She ought to remember him. She had seen him nearly every day for over fifteen years.

Cate rushed to the laptop to slow the playback speed and to zoom in on his face as tears streamed down hers. And there it was, plain as day. It looked like his head had been shaved bald, but otherwise, it was him.

Mick Brady had been in their home. This morning. He was alive.

Time stood still as Cate sat frozen for a long while. She didn't know what to do and couldn't think clearly. Her body was trying to process what her mind now knew. She felt betrayed and disrespected. She had so many questions.

Once she had gathered her wits enough to dial her mobile phone, she placed a call to her brother. He didn't pick up until after several rings, which nearly gave Cate an anxiety attack. She needed him right away.

"Hey, sis," James said as he answered. "What's up?"

"James! I need you to come over immediately," Cate said. "It's an emergency!" she could hear the distress in her voice. It didn't even sound like her. The pitch was higher, and she was talking so fast that her words were garbled.

"Whoa, slow down," he said. "Is everyone okay? Anyone injured?"

"No, nothing like that... just come over right now. I

mean it, James Tatum. Get your ass over here as fast as you can."

"Okay, okay," James said. "I'll leave now. Give me about fifteen minutes." Then he hung up the phone.

Cate was still in her chair at the kitchen table, visibly shaking, when her brother let himself in with his key.

"My God, Cate," he said when he laid eyes on her. "What has happened to you?" He set his keys down on the entryway table and rushed over to his sister.

"Look!" Cate said, pointing to Mick's face on the screen of her open laptop.

"What are we looking at?" James asked.

Cate didn't answer at first. She was still crying, and it was hard for her to speak. "The surveillance cameras were delivered this morning and I managed to get them set up myself. I had gone into the office, but returned home because I had forgotten my laptop."

"Okay?" James said, a skeptical look on his face.

"When I got here, I noticed the back door was ajar. I figured Jilly had left it open. You know how she is about that."

"I do," James said, still looking skeptical but allowing himself to chuckle a bit. "So?"

"I decided to check the footage before heading back to work... And I found... this..." Cate said, her hand trembling as she pointed at the screen. "It's him. Mick is alive."

James leaned forward to get a closer look. "That can't be," he muttered. "There's no way. I mean..."

"I know," Cate said. "It doesn't seem real. But it is. The proof is right in front of our faces."

James pushed play on the footage and watched, just as Cate had. He saw the guy walking in casually. And he saw Meesha amble up to the man, happy to see him. He looked at the time stamp and then checked his watch.

"This must be edited, Cate," he said. "There's no other explanation. Someone must be trying to toy with you."

"Damn it, James," Cate said, anger rising in her throat. She was in no mood to act polite or to hold back on what she wanted to say. "I was gone barely an hour this morning. Who would have had time to orchestrate this?"

"There's no need to raise your voice with me, Cate," her brother said, taking a step back and crossing his arms over his chest like he does when he's defensive.

"There's more you still don't know," Cate continued. "And frankly, this fits in. It's all beginning to make sense."

"What are you talking about?" James asked. "I am, honest to God, concerned about you, Cate. You haven't been acting like yourself lately. I thought you just needed some time, but this is extreme. What, are you going to tell the kids their father is alive after they buried him in that cemetery two weeks ago? If you can't come to your own senses, think of the kids."

"James, I love you, but stop belittling me and talking down to me like I'm a child who doesn't know what she's doing."

James shook his head and stepped a few feet away. He raised both hands in the air out of exasperation. "Just answer one question for me then," he said. "If you think your husband is alive, why in the hell have you been sleeping with Neil Fredericks?"

Tears began to flow harder and faster down Cate's face. Of all the things to sort through, her relationship with Neil was the one that would cause her the most pain. She had thought her husband was dead and buried. She never in a million years would have gotten romantically involved with another man if she had known Mick was still alive. Yet she had real feelings for Neil. Their relationship was growing stronger, and she thought they might have a future together. She wished her brother would have more compassion and not throw this dilemma in her face so callously.

"Do you remember me telling you about Pal, the homeless man who sits outside of my building?" Cate asked.

"Yes, I do," James said. "You buy a breakfast sandwich and a cup of coffee for him every morning. I know the story. What's that got to do with anything?"

"After I thought Mick was dead, Pal muttered something that disturbed me one morning. He said he had seen Mick talking to Tim Negley, the owner of Lorraine's Diner."

"Okay. And?"

"I tried to put it out of my mind, but what Pal had said kept bugging me and I couldn't let it go. Yesterday morning, I went to Lorraine's myself and paid Tim a visit."

James sat down in a chair at the kitchen table next to his sister. He was becoming more interested in her theory as it started to sound more plausible. "Go on," he said.

"I made small talk at first, mentioning how our parents used to be friends with his mom, Lorraine. But then I flat out asked him if he knew anything that could help me make sense out of Pal's comment. He acted cagey when he heard Mick's name."

"Really?" James asked, narrowing his eyes.

"Yeah," Cate continued. "Tim was hiding something. He tried to dismiss me, but I followed him back towards the kitchen and finally got his attention again. And when I did, he pulled me to the side and whispered that I was out of my depth and should leave it alone."

"Holy shit," James said, leaning back in his chair and placing both hands on his head. He was thinking. "Do the detectives working your case know about this?"

"No, not as far as I know," Cate replied. "Detective Hemming hasn't mentioned it. And well, Neil and I don't talk about the case when we see each other. Why?"

James tapped one index finger along the top of his head as if he were debating whether to tell Cate everything he knew. "I've been trying to look into things like you asked," he said. "Luke Hemming has pretty much frozen me out. I haven't been able to get anything useful from him. He knows I'm sniffing around and he doesn't want you receiving preferential treatment."

"I get that," Cate said. "But what I now know rises to a level such that I must find out what's going on. I can't sit around and wait for the police to investigate for me. Especially…"

"Especially because Luke Hemming wants to bring you in under arrest," James said, finishing his sister's sentence.

"Exactly," Cate said. "I'd like to think it would be as simple as showing Detective Hemming this evidence to exonerate me, but I'd first like to find out what Mick is involved in and why he would fake his own death. If he's in some kind of danger and was forced to do it, I could never forgive myself if I blew things for him and caused his actual death. We need to understand what's happening before we tell Detective Hemming anything. There's too much potential for confusion."

"Same goes for Neil Fredericks," James added.

The two of them sat quietly for several moments as they each thought about what to do.

"Look, I'll go down and talk to Tim Negley," James said. "I have to tread lightly so as not to interfere with Detective Hemming's investigation. But I'll see what I can find out."

"Good," Cate said, sounding relieved. "I'm going with you."

27

The breakfast crowd at Lorraine's had thinned out by the time Cate and James arrived and the lunch rush had not yet begun. The sun was climbing higher in the sky now and the air outdoors was warming up. Cate knew Tim wouldn't want to cooperate, but it seemed like a good time to catch him. A chime above the front door dinged as she and her brother walked inside. It was a day for moving fast. Neither Cate nor James had any interest in dragging things out. They needed answers, and they needed them right away.

Kai was there, working behind the counter. She recognized Cate from the morning prior.

"Hi," Kai said in her cheerful voice. "Two for breakfast?"

"Hello, Kai," Cate said. "We're just here to speak with Tim Negley. This is my brother James. He's an officer with the Rosemary Run Police Department." James flashed his badge and a reserved smile.

"Oh, yes, Miss. I'll get him right away," Kai said as she

turned to head for the kitchen and the back office. It was obvious James made her nervous. In less than two minutes, she returned to the front with news that Tim was unavailable.

"That's not a surprise," Cate said under her breath.

"I'm sorry, Miss. Cate," Kai said. Cate was pleased the young waitress remembered her name. Maybe Tim had mentioned it.

James was getting frustrated. Cate noticed he had balled up one fist. His body was tense and he was ready to take action. "Forget it," James said to Kai. "I'll go to him. That way, Tim doesn't have to stop what he's doing to walk up front." Cate's eyebrows rose at her brother's gall. She was glad to see him taking charge like this.

"Oh, no, no, no," Kai said. "I can't let you go back..." But James was already through the kitchen door. Cate followed closely behind.

James stomped loudly as he made his way into the kitchen, looking for Tim's office. When he found it, he banged on the door and then let himself in without waiting. "Tim Negley," James said when he laid eyes on the man. Cate positioned herself just outside the office so she could watch for anyone trying to intervene. She would make sure that her brother was not interrupted.

"Who are you? And what do you want?" Tim said, his voice echoing throughout the small kitchen. Cate thought he sounded afraid. And she thought he should. Employees were beginning to notice what was happening. Several had congregated together and were listening while they discussed whether to leave their posts until it was over.

"I'm Officer James Tatum with the Rosemary Run

Police Department. And I'm Cate Brady's brother. You know our parents, Ron and Ellen Tatum."

"Oh," Tim said.

"Good. Now we're all caught up." James leaned over Tim's desk so far he could have grabbed the man with both hands if he wanted to. "I understand my sister asked you some questions yesterday morning. But you didn't give her any answers."

Tim squirmed in his seat. He looked like he was about to crawl out of his skin he was so uncomfortable.

"What's wrong? Cat got your tongue?" James asked as he leaned closer. "Maybe you need some... encouragement. You know, to convince you to talk. Huh?" Cate had never seen her brother like this. It was quite a thrill. She was impressed.

"No..." Tim stammered, putting both palms out towards James and lowering his voice to a whisper. "I can't. They've got eyes and ears all over this place." He shook his head, trying to collect himself. "Here's what I can say. Watch the bar next door tonight-- Wingman's Pub. Park around back by the dumpsters. Go in and order a few beers so you don't look suspicious. Around nine o'clock, go outside like you're leaving the property, then get into your car, kill your engine, and wait. You'll get your answers."

"I'd better," James said. "Or I'm coming back."

28

"He's scared to death of something," James said as he and Cate got back into the car. "Or someone."

"I agree," Cate replied. "What do you make of it?"

"It's hard to say," James said. "But if this is somehow related to a gang or other organized crime, it might explain why someone would try and fake their own death to get out of it. Those types of organizations don't just let you go when you want to leave. Sometimes, you don't even have a choice about getting involved with them in the first place."

"So, you're saying what Mick did might have been justified?"

"I don't know yet," James said as he put the car into gear and drove out of the parking lot. "But I'm going to Wingman's tonight to investigate. You should stay home and watch the kids. We don't need you putting yourself in unnecessary danger."

Cate knew her brother was right. Aaron, Jilly, and Niko needed her. If whatever Mick was involved in was serious enough that he'd had to fake his death, Cate and the kids should stay far away from it. But she couldn't help being curious. She began to wonder again if she had underestimated the seriousness of the threat.

"James, do you think the kids and I are in any danger?" she asked. "We know it was Mick in the house this morning because we caught him on camera..."

"We don't know that for sure and we won't unless we see a living, breathing Mick. Let's not get ahead of ourselves," James explained as he turned his car onto Flock Hollow Lane towards Cate's house to drop her off at home. She wasn't ready to be left alone just yet. "As for your safety, I'm not sure what to think right now," her brother continued. "You should take extra precautions."

"Hey!" Cate said, suddenly thinking about solutions. "We could have Mick's grave exhumed. Then we'd find out that his body wasn't there. Do you think the casket is empty? Oh... or maybe someone else's body is in his place. That would be creepy. Also, we could dig deeper, pun intended, into the medical examiner who signed his death certificate."

"Yeah," her brother answered. "That's all true. But if we want to protect Mick, we don't want to draw attention to this thing. At least, not until we know more. How about you leave the investigating to me?"

Cate laughed. It was probably comical to hear her rattling on about investigation tactics based on nothing more than the crime television she'd watched over the years. "Right," she said. "I guess that is your job. I know you're good at it."

As James pulled into Cate's driveway, she was a ball of

nerves. She was afraid to stay at home alone, although she didn't want to let on. And she was a little afraid to run into Mick. What would they say to each other, after all? She wondered what exactly would go down at Wingman's tonight. And she wanted desperately to call Neil and tell him what had happened.

"Would you like me to come inside and look around?" James asked. "I don't mind."

"No," Cate replied. "I'm a big girl. I can always call if I need you. And I have the handgun. If someone tries to hurt me, I'll use it."

"Okay, then," James said, patting his sister on the knee. "We will get to the bottom of this. I promise. You hang in there a while longer."

Cate was glad that, finally, James would find out what was really going on. She wanted nothing more than to figure it out and to put this nightmare behind her, one way or another.

29

"I have some news," Detective Luke Hemming said to his partner. They were eating lunch at their desks, watching an episode of a cop drama on Neil's computer as they chewed on sandwiches and drank cold cans of cola from the vending machine.

"Yeah?" Neil asked.

"I'm ready to make an arrest in the Mick Brady case."

"Oh, really?" Neil asked, fidgeting in his seat as he imagined Cate being brought into the station in handcuffs. "Who?"

"The wife. It's almost always the wife. You know that." Luke stared intently at his partner and took some pleasure in watching his distress. Luke thought Neil needed to be taught a lesson about getting close to a suspect. It was bad form and it never should have happened. Luke intended to see that it never happened again. Not on his watch.

Neil cleared his throat and tried to keep his voice level. "Did you turn up something I don't know about? Because the evidence I've seen is all circumstantial. It's not enough to make an arrest."

"That, I did," Luke said, sounding pleased with himself.

"Well, what is it?" Neil asked.

"Detective Fredericks, I mean no disrespect, but I'm aware of your relationship with the suspect. I'm sure you'll understand why I am no longer comfortable sharing details of this case with you. I'm going to talk to the chief and request you be reassigned."

30

Cate recognized Neil's number when her mobile phone rang. She was sitting at the kitchen table in her house, watching the security camera footage over and over again. She wasn't sure she should tell Neil about any of this. There were complications now that she knew Mick was alive. Both personally and as related to the case. Cate realized that the situation she found herself in was precarious. If she made a wrong move and acted like she was hiding something, it could lead to her own arrest and possibly even conviction. On the flip side, if she divulged too much to the authorities, it could mean blowing Mick's cover and placing him in harm's way.

After four rings with Neil waiting on the line, Cate answered, just before the call went to voicemail. "Hello, Neil," she said, her voice a mixture of tenderness and reserve.

"Cate!" he said. "I need to talk to you right away. But not in any of our usual spots. Is there somewhere you can meet me?"

"Sure, I guess," she replied. "What's this all about?"

"I'll tell you when I see you. Where?"

"There's a restaurant on the other side of town I haven't been to in a long time…" Cate said.

"That won't work," Neil interrupted. "It has to be somewhere private, where we won't be seen or heard. It can't be your house and it can't be mine."

Cate thought for a moment. She wasn't in the habit of sneaking around, so she wasn't very good at it. "Okay, I know a place," she said. "We can meet at my parents' house. In their barn. They won't mind."

"Good," Neil said. "Their place is out on Pleasant Valley Road, right?"

"Yes, that's right," Cate confirmed. "I can be there in about twenty minutes."

Cate gathered her things to leave the house for the third time that day. She had already texted Laura to let her know she wouldn't be back in the office. She had far too much on her mind to concentrate on work.

The weather was still nice as she drove into Ron and Ellen's driveway. It was a stark contrast from the raging storm which had been happening the last time she was here. The weather seemed almost too perfect. Cate thought about how it wasn't right that the earth kept turning as if nothing was wrong on the days when ordinary lives were devastated.

Neil hadn't arrived yet, so Cate stopped in the house to make sure her parents were at work. Neither were home, so she locked everything back up and headed down to the barn, allowing Joey to tag along. The hired help had already been there and gone for the day, leaving the place empty aside from the Tatum's animals. After saying hello to the animals and taking a look at the storm damage repair, Cate got settled in at a picnic table in the barn and waited for her lover to arrive. She thought about the man her dad had chased off the night of the storm and she wondered if it had been Mick. Her dad's statement about the man not seeming aggressive had continued to stand out in her mind. She guessed it would make sense for it to have been Mick if he had, in fact, been watching over the family. Perhaps he was just checking in to make sure they were okay.

Before she could get too lost in her own thoughts, Neil's car sped down the gravel road and came to a stop next to Cate's, outside of her parents' red barn. Neil got out in a hurry and rushed to Cate, taking her into his arms and kissing her deeply. She had considered refraining from physical contact, but he scooped her up so fast and so passionately that she didn't have time to resist. She didn't want to resist.

"Cate, my love," Neil said once their lips parted. He had never called Cate his love before. It made her go weak in the knees. "Luke Hemming knows about us. He's having me pulled from the case."

Neil was talking so fast that Cate didn't have a chance to mention her big news. "What?" She asked. "What does that mean for..."

"I hurried to meet you because Luke says he has enough evidence to make an arrest. To arrest *you*."

"That's impossible," Cate said.

"I thought so, too," Neil said. "I told Luke that, as far as I knew, all the evidence against you was circumstantial and wasn't enough to justify making an arrest. But he says he found something. He wouldn't tell me what it was."

"But, really," Cate said. "It's impossible. Listen to what I'm telling you."

Neil lowered his eyebrows and a look of confusion spread across his face. "What am I missing?" he asked.

Cate took Neil's hands in hers and stepped close to him, whispering into his ear. She wasn't sure why she was doing it that way. It's not like anyone would overhear them out there. Unless Mick was hiding nearby. But she thought that was unlikely. More likely, was that Cate couldn't bear to look in Neil's eyes when she said the words.

"It's a long story," she began. "And I'll tell you all the details you want. But James and I have reason to believe Mick is still alive."

"Still alive?" Neil asked, shocked. He wanted to pull back from Cate's embrace and look her in the eye, but he didn't. "That means…"

"It means a lot of things," Cate said. "But first and foremost, it means there's no way I could have murdered him because no murder took place."

"That's right," Neil said, getting excited. "I've got to go. I've got to stop them from arresting you." He turned and began to head for his car. His movements were becoming frantic. He was rattled by everything that was happening.

"Not so fast!" Cate said, reaching out a hand and pulling him back to her. "We don't know what's going on yet, but we think Mick may have been in grave danger and that's why he faked his own death. For all we know, he did it to protect me and the kids. We can't let anyone else know he's alive until we find out what's happening."

"And just how do you plan to do that?" Neil asked, exasperated.

"We have a lead. James will check it out tonight," Cate said.

"Cate, I don't think you understand," Neil pleaded, desperately. "Luke is ready to make an arrest. He might arrest you before James pursues that lead tonight. Luke won't tell me any more about it, so I can't be sure. But we need to stop it from happening. Once you're arrested, it will be on your record forever. Think of your kids."

"I am thinking of my kids," Cate replied with certainty. "I need you to buy me time. Just give me until tomorrow somehow. Let us see what we can find out. A man on good authority to know told James that we would have all of our answers tonight if he watched the bar at Wingman's Pub. It's out on the ridge next to Lorraine's."

Neil began paced back-and-forth on the dirt floor as Joey looked on. He wanted to do what was best for Cate and her kids. He was upset to learn that Mick was alive because it probably meant that Cate would go back to her husband. Neil had grown to care deeply for Cate in a short time and couldn't imagine the thought of losing her. But regardless of how things turned out for him personally, he knew he would do anything for her. It wasn't even a question anymore.

"Okay," he said, walking back to Cate and putting his arms around her waist. Touching her was presumptuous now, but she was hard to resist.

Cate's insides stirred as she pressed herself against

Neil and felt the heat coming off of his body. The feelings confused her. She wondered how she could desire another man when she knew that her husband was alive. Neil could tell what she was thinking, so he saved her the trouble of making any difficult decisions. At least, for now.

"Just promise me you'll let James handle this lead tonight," Neil said. "You're not trying to go after him, are you?"

Cate hesitated before she spoke. She was choosing her words carefully. "I know I should stay home with the kids," she replied. "I'm not trained for this sort of thing."

"Good," Neil said, satisfied with her answer. "We'll talk again soon. Be ever so careful."

31

By the time evening arrived and darkness fell on Rosemary Run, Cate had already made up her mind. She tidied up the house, then baked a chicken casserole and ate dinner with Aaron, Jilly, and Niko. The four of them enjoyed a leisurely meal together, discussing things that were happening at school and reviewing tomorrow night's plans for Halloween. Cate looked at each one of her children. She really looked at them. She considered what they had been through in the past couple of weeks and how resilient they had shown themselves to be. She thought about what their lives might be like if their father somehow came back home. And she thought about what their lives might be like if they somehow lost their mother.

After dinner, Cate waited until she was sure James had already left home, then she called Rebecca to ask if she'd mind coming over to sit with the kids. Once she knew her sister-in-law was on the way, Cate went into her bedroom and pulled out the handgun that she and Mick had stashed in the top of the closet. She ran her finger over the cold, metal barrel and then looked at herself in the mirror as she pretended to aim and fire a shot. The moment Rebecca arrived, Cate slipped the handgun into her bag, kissed the kids goodbye, and headed for Wingman's Pub.

Cate turned off all the lights on her SUV as she pulled into the parking lot at Lorraine's Diner and slipped into a spot out back. The supper crowd had already receded and there weren't many people left inside the building. In fact, Cate noticed that there weren't many people out at all that evening. It was almost eerie. She thought maybe people were staying in tonight because they had plans to be out tomorrow for Halloween. Maybe they were home making costumes or carving jack-o'-lanterns. It was already perfect weather for trick-or-treating: clear and cool with a brightly lit full moon. Cate hoped the weather would hold on through tomorrow.

From where she had parked at the diner, Cate could see the back of Wingman's Pub, including the dumpsters Tim had mentioned. She squinted to be sure and was able to identify James sitting in his car and watching the back door. It was almost eight o'clock and she knew her brother would be going inside soon to order a beer, just like Tim had told him to. Cate intended to stay put and observe along with him. She didn't need her brother's permission to be there.

Cate held her position in her vehicle and waited for over an hour before she saw anything other than James walking inside. It was cold, and even though she had worn a turtleneck and a thick sweater to keep warm, the bite was getting to her. When she saw a group of intimidating businessmen walk around the back of the building, she decided it was the perfect time to get out for a closer look. She figured moving around would help her warm up, anyway. To be sure she was protected, Cate carefully loaded a round of bullets into the handgun, then secured the weapon in a strap attached to her ankle. She stepped out of her SUV quietly, taking care to lock the doors by hand and to close them very gently.

Cate walked gingerly along the grassy embankment at the back of the parking lot that was shared by Lorraine's and Wingman's, save for a narrow median. She was soon able to get a better look at the businessmen behind the pub, thanks to the light of the moon. There were six or eight men there total. Too many to count until she got a little closer. As she took step after step, she could hear their voices, too, and she could begin to make out what they were saying. It was something about a deal. They were making an exchange. There were seven of them. That was the number. She looked hard at each one as she continued to approach, wondering if any one of them was her husband. As she stepped closer and closer, one calculated step at a time, it suddenly became apparent to Cate what was happening. They were making a drug deal.

Oh no, she thought.

She wondered what she had gotten herself into. Beyond that, she wondered what Mick had gotten himself into. Distracted by her worries, Cate made an innocent misstep and tripped on an uneven piece of pavement. Her boot became wedged and she let out a gasp as she stumbled and nearly fell on her face.

"Someone's there," one of the men growled angrily.

"It's a woman," another one said. "We don't know what she heard. We can't let her get away!"

In a dizzying blur of adrenaline and terror, several of the men swarmed around Cate and hoisted her up off the ground. One of them, who smelled like cigars and whiskey, placed his hand over her mouth before she had a chance to cry for help. Cate's very life flashed before her eyes as the men dragged her further towards the back of the pub building. She'd always been told to never let an attacker take you to another location. Because if they did, your chances of escaping with your life were slim to none. Cate didn't know what these men might do with her, but scenes of being tied up in a dingy room or thrown into the trunk of a car flooded her mind. She tried to look for James, hoping that he would come back outside and save her. But he was nowhere to be found. The understanding settled over Cate in a wash. She needed to fight with everything she had, right there and now, if she ever wanted to see her kids again.

Listening to her instincts, Cate launched a counter-attack. She began biting, scraping, and bucking around with all of her energy and strength. She was outnumbered by the men, but they were taken aback with her feistiness. Within moments, she managed to wriggle free. Seeing an opening to escape, Cate started to run back towards the diner and towards the safety of her SUV. She had barely made it halfway when she heard him call out her name.

It was definitely him. She'd know his voice anywhere.

"Cate!" he called.

Frozen in place now with what felt like the weight of the world on her shoulders, Cate was uncertain as to whether or not she would be able to move. She knew that once she turned around and saw his face, things could never go back to the way they were. Not even in her dreams. Yet, she also knew that she could never truly move forward if she didn't see him with her own eyes. It was a critical juncture.

Compelled by the inevitability of it all, Cate slowly turned around. And laid her eyes on her husband.

32

It had only been two weeks, but Mick looked to Cate like an entirely different person than the one she had known and loved. His head was bald and he looked thin, like he had lost weight. She wondered what had happened to him. She could hardly believe this was real.

"Cate," he said again, softer this time. The businessmen with him were breaking away and heading back inside the pub. Cate continued to stare at her husband, but she didn't run to him. They stood several feet apart. "I know how this looks, but you must get out of here. I had to fake my death to protect you and the kids."

"To protect us?" Cate asked. "I would have liked to have made that decision for myself. Do you have any idea what you've put us through?"

"I know," Mick said, taking a step closer to his wife. "I need you to trust me. I wouldn't have done this unless it was the only way. I dropped by to check in on you and I will always watch out for you. But I can't do that if we're both dead, which is exactly what will happen if you don't leave right away."

"You don't look good," Cate said. "Has something happened to you?"

Before Mick could answer, the businessmen returned, spilling through the back door of the pub building. A look of terror spread across Mick's face. He knew that they'd gone to check with the boss. Their return meant that the boss was not pleased and intended to tie up loose ends.

"What is this?" one of the men asks. "Is she with you?" he continued, pointing at Cate angrily. "Because this isn't how things were supposed to go tonight. We like to keep our hands clean. No complications."

"She didn't mean any harm," Mick said. "And she didn't see anything. She won't be a problem, I promise."

"That's the thing," another one of the men added. "A clean operation means no witnesses. No exceptions." He paused for a moment and rubbed his fat thumb and index finger along his temples until he reached a decision. "Take her inside, boys. We will deal with her there."

Cate turned and tried with all her might to run again, but the men were too fast and they caught up with her effortlessly. She scolded herself for taking the time to stop and talk to Mick. She hadn't learned anything new. She could have gotten away to safety if she had kept running and had not turned around when he'd called her name. The men overpowered Cate and, despite protests from Mick, took her into the bar and shoved her into a dimly lit back room. Before she could get her bearings, a large man with an air of authority stomped into the room. He was in charge.

"Mr. Brady," the man began, pacing the floor. "I'm not sure you realize just how pissed off I am about this conflict. I was assured a smooth operation, and this has turned into anything but. You've given me no choice. There's only one way to handle this now."

"Anything," Mick pleaded, dropping to his knees. "I'll do anything you want. Just let her go. I promise you she won't be a problem."

The surly boss put his hands on his hips and let out a hearty belly laugh. The sound of his voice made Cate shudder. Everything about his demeanor told her he was a really bad guy. This danger was on an entirely different level than anything she had ever brushed with in the past. It made her terribly afraid for her husband, for herself, and for their innocent children who were at home with their aunt having no idea the peril their parents faced.

"I'm pleased to hear that," the boss snapped at Mick. "Because that's exactly the kind of allegiance I require." He walked over to Mick, then pulled a pistol out of his coat and handed it to him. "Shoot her."

Cate yelled out in fear, her composure leaving her. The situation felt surreal, like a bad dream. She struggled to wrap her mind around it.

"What did you say?" Mick asked.

"You heard me. Shoot the woman. She's nothing but a liability."

Everyone in the room stood silently for a tense moment. Even the other businessmen seemed nervous about what was going to transpire. Mick looked around the room at the reprehensible characters he had gotten involved with, then he looked at his good and kind wife.

He knew that turning on the boss would mean retribution from others in the organization. He knew he would need to eliminate every last man present to get away. And he knew there would be a record of him having been with them tonight, which meant they'd be looking for him. But the only people who knew his wife had been here were standing in this room.

Without hesitation, Mick turned towards the boss and placed a bullet squarely between his eyes. In a flurry of motion, he then did the same as he shot the others, one by one, all except a single remaining businessman who had found enough time to lunge towards him, knocking the gun out of his hands. Mick maintained a strong grip on the weapon as the man pushed him back into a wall and worked feverishly to save himself. Wanting to help and figuring she had nothing to lose, Cate jumped in and attempted to choke the man from behind.

The three of them wrestled for what felt like an eternity. Mick and Cate would think they had the upper hand until the businessman would make a sudden move, regaining the advantage. Cate was beginning to exhaust herself and it looked like Mick was too, when, heroically, James and Neil burst through the door, coming to the rescue. Their weapons were raised, and they were ready to save the day. James squared up his aim and took a shot, which landed in the agitated businessman's head. The man collapsed onto the ground, releasing Cate and Mick as his body went limp and his eyes became vacant.

"Cate! Are you okay?" Neil asked, rushing to her side.

"Sis, you good?" James echoed.

"I'm fine," Cate said, pushing herself to a standing

position despite feeling disoriented. "Just a little shaken up."

When she caught her breath, Cate found herself standing equidistant between Neil and Mick. It was a position she never in her wildest dreams thought she would find herself in. The chemistry between Cate and Neil was palpable. She couldn't have hidden it if she tried.

The sound of police sirens rang out from the front of the building, and none other than Luke Hemming made his way to the back room. He burst through the door, gun raised, like his colleagues before him.

"What the hell happened in here?" Luke asked, lowering his weapon when he saw that there wasn't a threat.

"You first, Hemming," James said. "What are you doing here?"

"I happened to be driving by and saw Neil's car out front. I wanted to tell my partner there have been new developments in the Mick Brady case. So, I pulled into the parking lot just as people began fleeing from the building and saying they'd heard gunshots in the back."

"Yeah?" James asked. "Well, I've got a development in the Mick Brady case for you. Here he is in the flesh. My sister didn't murder her husband. Because he isn't even dead."

"I know she didn't," Luke said. "The evidence I thought I had came back a dud. It was related to another Cate Brady who was the same age and had the same middle initial. But the prints didn't match."

Cate let out an audible sigh of relief. She could feel

her shoulders relax as she leaned her head back and said a silent prayer of thanks.

"I also attempted to exhume Mr. Brady's body and found out his casket was empty," Luke added, his voice softer and kinder. "I looked into Mr. Brady's record with the military. I could see that he was a good guy. A patriot and a model citizen. I knew there had to be more to the story." Luke's lips turned down at the corners as if he were saddened by Mick's plight. "I came here to tell Neil that his friend was off the hook."

"Wait," Mick said. "Cate was being investigated for my murder?"

"Indeed she was," Detective Hemming said. "I thought I had quite a case on her, too. All circumstantial though. In retrospect, I should have been more careful. I was too eager to be an instrument of justice. My ego got in the way." He turned towards Cate. "Mrs. Brady, I'm sorry for what I've put you through. I hope you can forgive me."

"Thank you for saying that, Detective Hemming," Cate replied. She turned to her husband. "You're amongst friends here, Mick. These men will let you walk out the door when we're done and disappear if that's what you choose to do."

"If I'm going to keep you and the kids safe, that's what I *have* to do," Mick clarified. "I don't have any choice in the matter. These are very bad guys. Their associates will know it was me and they will look for me. Hard. The only saving grace here is that no one outside of the present company knows you were here. You can go home and live your life without having to worry about them coming after you." Cate felt like she'd been punched in the gut when she heard her husband refer to her life without him in it.

"How did you get involved with these people?" Cate asked. "And how did you hide it from me? You must have been dealing with them for quite some time. Otherwise, things wouldn't have reached the point where the only out was faking your own death."

Mick wiped beads of perspiration off his forehead as he spoke to his wife. He hadn't wanted her to know his secrets. He hadn't wanted to hurt her. "It started not long after we moved back to Rosemary Run," Mick explained. "In fact, it was why we moved back. Some guys from an international crime organization sought me out and strong-armed me. They knew I needed money, and they offered me a solution. I didn't want to participate and I tried to avoid them, but once they locked on, they were like bulldogs. They told me they would hurt you and the kids if I didn't cooperate. They wanted to funnel cash through my consulting business. They gave me a cut. But I swear, I didn't have a choice. It was horrible being beholden to them."

"Pardon the interruption," Detective Hemming said. "What is the name of this international crime organization?"

"I'm sorry, Detective, but I can't tell you that," Mick said. "I can't leave any trace that might lead back to Cate." Mick could tell that Luke didn't like that answer. "Do you have a family, Detective Hemming?" Mick asked. Luke nodded affirmatively. "Then I don't need to explain my motivations to you. Please find another way. You have plenty of evidence on this floor with which to do so."

"Mick," Cate said softly, reaching up and touching her husband for the first time since he had come back. "You changed your look."

Cate had always felt an affection for her husband's head. She had thought there was something special about a strong man making his head vulnerable. Cate believed it an honor to be trusted with Mick's physical person. She remembered the countless times Mick had laid his head in her lap while she gently stroked his hair. It cut her like a knife to see his head bald.

Feeling Cate's soft, familiar touch and hearing her comment made Mick emotional. "I didn't want to tell you…" he said, hot tears collecting in his eyes.

"Tell me what?" Cate asked. "I think we've reached the point of putting it all out on the table here, wouldn't you say?" Seeming to sense what was coming, James stepped forward and put a hand on his sister's shoulder.

"Okay… I… There's no easy way to say this…" Mick muttered. "I have stage four pancreatic cancer," he continued slowly, trying not to crumble into a sobbing mess. "I've known since before we left Connecticut. I wanted to get you home to Rosemary Run where you would have family around. And it's the reason I went along with the crime organization. They gave me money to pay for experimental cancer treatment. I even borrowed from my mom. I was willing to do anything to stay alive and to find a cure. Most people with my disease don't last this long. When it became clear the treatment wasn't working and I knew my time was coming to an end, I staged this scenario to make sure you and the kids were okay before I... Went away for good..." His voice trailed off.

"Oh, Mick," Cate said, wrapping her arms around her husband's neck and placing one hand on the back of his bald head. Tears streamed down her face as it all began to make so much sense. Mick was loyal to a fault. Cate had always known Mick would do anything for her and the kids. Her deepest fear had been that her husband was hiding something from her. She should have realized he was doing so for all the right reasons.

"I wanted the kids to, you know, remember me the way I was," Mick continued, holding on tightly to his wife. "And you, too," he said to Cate. "I've done my research and I've talked to palliative care doctors. The end stages of this disease are horrible. I'd rather we said goodbye now, before I become a shadow of my former self."

"So your bald head? And your weakness?" Cate asked, fighting to maintain her composure. She had noticed during the struggle with the businessman that Mick wasn't nearly as strong as he used to be.

"I tried a last-ditch effort with a new kind of chemo," Mick said. "It isn't working."

The pain of her husband's situation made Cate feel like she had been turned inside out and all the raw, sensitive parts were exposed. She thought this might be worse than the death Mick had conjured up. She finally understood why he'd done it.

"Your mom came to me about your debt to her," Cate said. "And she told me she loaned you the money for the down payment on our mortgage. I didn't understand..."

"I know," Mick replied. "I've been watching over the

house for the past couple of weeks and I found out that Mom had hired somebody to break in and steal financial records, then make it look like it was a robbery."

"That was your *mom?*" Detective Hemming asked, surprised.

"Yeah, it was," Mick confirmed. "Grief makes people do strange things. Mom found some of my medical bills even though I thought I had gotten rid of them all. I approached her just the other day and explained everything. We came to an understanding and healed some old wounds." He turned towards his wife and looked her in the eye. "Cate, she won't give you any more trouble. She's backing off on the debt. She's paying off our house in full, anonymously. The deed will be in your name alone and you'll have no worries. I've made arrangements for my life insurance to go to Nancy when I..." He couldn't finish the sentence. "She'll be repaid in full."

"I'm flabbergasted," Cate said. "I didn't know that woman had it in her. But I'm grateful she does."

"She's sorry, Cate," Mick affirmed. "She truly is. And that's not all. She has offered to be with me. You know, at the end. She's my mom. She was with me when I came into this world and I guess it's only fitting that she be with me when I leave it."

There wasn't a dry eye left in the room as the group of them felt the Brady family's pain. It was heartbreaking. And they were out of time. Sirens began in the distance then grew louder. They all knew the place would soon be swarming with additional police officers.

"To those of you who were never here," Detective Hemming announced. "This is your cue to leave." He didn't make eye contact with James or Neil. He knew they wouldn't breathe a word of what they had witnessed tonight. "As far as I'm concerned," Luke continued. "Detective Fredericks and I were meeting here for a drink when we heard gunshots coming from the back room. We arrived to find an apparent shootout amongst warring members of a criminal gang. And that's the end of the story. Mrs. Brady, get back to your home where you've been all evening with your brother, please."

Cate nodded her understanding.

"And Mr. Brady," Luke said, choking up as he addressed Mick. "Good luck to you, sir. Godspeed."

Cate and Mick knew it was time to say goodbye. For good. They both knew Mick would disappear for real as he journeyed to the place where he'd spend the remainder of his days. They turned and embraced each other one last time.

"How will I know...?" Cate asked as she pressed her cheek tightly against her husband's.

"Mom will let you know."

"Can I contact you?" she asked.

"It's too risky. I won't jeopardize your safety," Mick said emphatically.

Sirens continued to grow louder and Cate knew that this was the end. She placed her hands on the sides of her husband's bald head and looked him in the eye. "Mick Brady, I have loved you every single day since I met you. You have given me more happiness in fifteen years than many people experience in an entire lifetime. You've been the best father to our kids. You will live on in the three of them. I'll see to that. Thank you for the life we shared."

"The feeling is mutual, my dear Cate," Mick replied, sobbing with big heaves now. "You are my entire life. You've made it worth living."

"Oh, Mick," Cate sputtered.

Then Mick Brady kissed his wife on the lips softly. He turned and walked out the back door, making one final comment to Detective Fredericks as he passed by. "Neil," Mick said with the weight of life itself in his voice. "You take good care of her."

THE END.

———

Get the next book in the series:

Her Hidden Past
Rosemary Run - Book Two
kellyutt.com

ENJOY THIS BOOK?

A NOTE FROM AUTHOR KELLY UTT

Did you enjoy this book? You can make a big difference.

Reviews are the most powerful tools in my arsenal when it comes to getting attention for my books. As much as I'd like to, I don't have the financial muscle of a New York publisher. I can't take out full page ads in the newspaper or put posters on the subway.

(Not yet, anyway.)

But I do have something much more effective than that, and it's something that those publishers would kill to get their hands on.

A committed and loyal group of readers.

Honest reviews of my books help bring them to the attention of other readers.

If you've enjoyed this book, I would be very grateful if you could spend just five minutes leaving a review (it can be as short as you like) on the book's Amazon page and on Goodreads or BookBub.

Thank you very much.

ALSO BY KELLY UTT

Have you read them all?

———

In the Rosemary Run Series

In the charming Northern California town of Rosemary Run, there's trouble brewing below the picture-perfect surface. Don't let the manicured lawns and stylish place settings fool you. Nothing is exactly as it seems. Secrets and lies threaten to upend the status quo and destroy lives when— not if— they're revealed.

BOOK 1 - HER DEEPEST FEAR

BOOK 2 - HER HIDDEN PAST

BOOK 3 - HER BOLDEST LIE

BOOK 4 - HER DARKEST HOUR

BOOK 5 - HER BURIED SECRET

BOOK 6 - HER WORST MISTAKE

———

In The Past Life Series

The Past Life Series chronicles the Hartmann and Davies families across time and space. This life-affirming story, anchored by the deep affection between George and Alessandra, reveals how the connections we share can ground us during even the most difficult times as we endeavor to learn what we're made of.

Join the family you'll feel like you already know as, together, they explore the meaning of life beyond what lies on the surface and fight to keep each other safe.

SHORT STORY PREQUEL - WAIT FOR OUR TURN

BOOK 1 - TELL ME I'M SAFE

BOOK 2 - SHOW ME THE DANGER

BOOK 3 - KEEP THEM FROM HARM

BOOK 4 - TAKE ME TO FIGHT

BOOK 5 - PICK UP THE PIECES

————

Be the first to know when new books are released by signing up for Kelly's e-mail list at www.kellyutt.com.

Kindle Unlimited Subscribers read for free.

ABOUT THE AUTHOR

STANDARDS OF STARLIGHT BOOKS
KELLY UTT

Kelly Utt writes emotional novels for readers who enjoy both suspense and sentimentality. She was born in Youngstown, Ohio in 1976.

Kelly grew up with a dad who would read a book on a weighty topic, ask her to read it, too, and then insist they discuss it together, igniting her passion for life's big questions. That passion is often reflected inKelly's novels, giving them a depth which leaves readers wanting more and thinking about her stories long after the last lines are read.

Kelly holds a Bachelor's degree in psychology from the

University of Tennessee, Knoxville and she studied graduate-level interactive media at Quinnipiac University.

She lives in the Nashville suburb of Franklin, Tennessee with her husband and sons.

www.kellyutt.com